Haley, Texas 1959

TWO NOVELLAS

DONLEY WATT

Haley, Texas 1959

TWO NOVELLAS

DONLEY WATT

CINCO PUNTOS PRESS
El Paso, Texas

FIRST EDITION
10 9 8 7 6 5 4 3 2 1

Library of Congress Cataloging-in-Publication Data

Watt, Donley.
Haley, Texas 1959 : two novellas / by Donley Watt. — 1st ed.
p. cm.
Contents: Haley, Texas 1959 — Seven days working.
ISBN 0-938317-48-2 (alk. paper)
1. East Texas—Social life and customs Fiction. 2. Teenage boys—East Texas Fiction. I. Watt, Donley. Seven days working. II. Title.
PS3573.A8585H3 1999
813'.54—dc21

99-37015
CIP

Photo of Donley Watt by Lynn Watt.
Cover art © 1999 by Charles Jones.

Dustjacket design by David Timmons.
(In memory of that old jokester, Bob Redman)

Thanks to the Texas Commission on the Arts
and to the Austin Writers' League.

Funded in part by

Always for Lynn

Other Books by Donley Watt

Can You Get There from Here?
The Journey of Hector Rabinal

Contents

Seven Days Working

Seven Days Working is a fictional narrative, an imaginative shaping and interweaving of both invented and actual events that occurred during those years when I was growing up in East Texas. This is my story, a purely personal and entirely subjective work of fiction. Some names have been changed, both place names and characters, and some have not. A number of the characters are composite rather than actual individuals. Some of the happenings have been dramatized, and time has arbitrarily been compressed or expanded, as I saw fit.

But the narrative is faithful to the emotional ground of my remembered truth, and reaches for even higher ground, that which lies hidden at the heart of all stories that matter, waiting to be discovered and illuminated.

—*Donley Watt*

Monday: Day 1

One Monday in June, the summer I turned fourteen, Daddy drove me over to a seventy-acre pasture he owned in Navarro County. He maneuvered our 1950 Ford sedan down a weed-ridden, double-rut road that led from a barbed wire gap on the north to a barbed wire gap on the south. This seventy acres was chock-full of second-growth mesquite trees—Daddy steered wide of the lacy leafed trees with their tire-spiking thorns. He guided the Ford off the road, easing it across the pasture and to a stop under a bois d'arc grove at the south fence line.

"Dadgum mesquites," he said. He pushed open the lid of a tin of tobacco with his thumb, filled his pipe. He clenched it in his jaw, but didn't light it. "Donnie, I want you to wipe 'em out."

He looked over at me—a skeptical look as I remember it. I gazed across the field of trees; they seemed to go on forever. "All of them?" I asked.

"If you don't get them all, it won't do any good. They'll come right back. A waste of time is all it'll be."

Daddy took a kitchen match from a box he kept on the seat beside him, dragged the blue tip across the sandpaper side of the box until the match flared. He lit his pipe, sucked on the stem two or three times until the tobacco glowed red hot, then pulled his wrist watch with its broken band out of the top pocket of his khaki shirt. He held it out and leaned back so he could read it. He shook his head. "Wasted most of a day already," he said. "You better get to work." And I stepped out into the heat and the glare of the Texas sun to begin seven days of work.

I didn't realize it then, but I was a poor third choice to fight the mesquite battle. For in 1954 there were a couple of more conventional ways to deal with those invasive, pesky trees. Both smacked of warfare: You could root-plow your field—hire a big dozer that dragged a row of two-foot long dagger-like plows behind. This took care of the mesquite, but the big Cat churned up everything in its path. It lay waste to your topsoil, burying it under waves of heavy clay and gravel. After root-plowing, a field took on the characteristics of the bombed-out strip of ground along the 38th parallel, that sorry piece of land that divided what had just become the two Koreas.

The second technique cost just as much, but was quicker. You could hire a wired-together biplane owned by an almost-ace WWII pilot who lived out towards Chatfield. He would, in a few swooping passes, dump enough herbicide on your place from his stubby yellow plane to frizzle every plant that dared to wave a green leaf.

Both of these methods took big bucks, and Daddy's cow-and-pasture math at its most optimistic couldn't justify the cost. Besides, quite simply, he didn't have the money. But he had me. And I was cheap.

That morning at Athens Feed and Seed north of the square, Daddy had bought me a double-bit axe with a hickory handle for

$3.95. The fellow who sold it to him eyed me up and down. His name was Goat; that was all I ever knew. Goat was a big man and appeared even bigger in the dim light of the feed store. With one arm he could swing a hundred-pound sack of horse and mule feed to his shoulder as if it were a pillow, and tote it to a pickup. Goat stood with the open doors at his back, the rays of sun spinning with streams of dust. He bounced the axe like a toy in his hand, then with a grin he spat a wad of Beechnut to one side, kicked it like a dog turd out the door. He wiped his mouth with the back of his hairy hand, then ran his finger down one edge of the axe, testing it for sharpness. "I don't reckon the boy'll wear it out," he said with a grin.

I slouched indifferently, but I tensed my right biceps as best I could, hoping Goat would take notice. I don't think he was impressed.

I'm fourteen, I wanted to say. I'll be playing football next fall. An Athens Hornet. Maybe "B" team, I conceded to myself, but football.

But it wasn't my place to say anything back. Daddy could have. He could have told Goat that I was big for my age—I was almost six feet tall, but awfully skinny—that I was strong or hardworking or at least willing. He could have stood up for me. But Daddy just laughed.

Goat started in on some joke, lowering his voice a little. I heard a couple of words—pussy and wiener. I wandered off, embarrassed to be hearing those words with Daddy around, embarrassed that Daddy grinned and leaned closer to listen.

Daddy was as decent and honest a man as ever lived in Henderson County, Texas. He was a deacon in the Church of Christ, would never even think to cheat on his income tax. He propped up various brothers-in-law when they were down and out. He was still sending a monthly check to his younger brother, who had been crippled by polio at age twelve and was finally about to get through the university.

Daddy was a good man, by any reckoning. But Daddy sure did like to hang around the real men, the profane ones. Not the lawyers and insurance salesmen and bankers and teachers, but the mechanics and weekend cowboys and welders—the men who worked with their hands and cussed and told off-color jokes and in other ways demonstrated an earthiness that Daddy must have always envied, but could never quite act out. Though maybe as a young man he had. For years later, when I was in the midst of a first wife/other woman crisis, he confessed (as a way to talk me back into a bad marriage) to a youthful indiscretion—in a West Texas oil camp before he married my mother. He would never forget how bad he felt afterwards.

After the joke, after Goat had done most of the laughing, Daddy, for another fifty cents, picked up a twelve-inch file so I could keep a fine edge on the axe's double blades. Daddy grew up working the cotton fields in Central Texas and preached the virtues of sharp tools. You just flat didn't work with dull tools, whether an axe or a hoe, whether chopping mesquite or chopping cotton.

Daddy showed me how to sink that axe in a corner fence post and work one edge of the blade with the file until it gleamed smooth, then work the axe free, and hone the other blade in the same way. He showed me how to hold the lower end of the file tight with one hand, and place my other hand, palm only, on the top end of the file, my fingers held out and away from the blade so not to slice off what someday might become a useful digit.

This seventy acres of mesquite-choked pasture that Daddy owned lay across the Trinity River thirty miles west of Athens, the small town I grew up in. At the Trinity River bridge, driving east to west, the land transforms, the deep East Texas sand hills give way to the black gumbo soil of Central Texas. Land that grows watermelons and tomatoes and barely supports bony-assed cows gives way to flat, black cotton land that sucks at your boots when it rains and cracks and curls like gray pieces of a warped puzzle in mid-summer.

The new synthetics had just about wiped out the cotton market so the best (and only) use for Daddy's seventy acres was to run a dozen or so brindle cows and a bull of questionable lineage. Lineage, whether for bulls or for kith and kin, was never the focus of our attention. "Sometimes it's better not to know," my mother would say. "Just accept what the Lord has given you."

"There's always somebody worse off," she would add as an afterthought.

Before the mesquite invaded, this old cotton land had been treeless for generations except for the grove of twisted bois d'arcs entrenched along the south fence line. The story goes that a bois d'arc tree provided the wood for the cross (yes, that cross), and ever since, the species has been cursed with crooked, twisted trunks and limbs so that it will never grow enough straight wood for another cross. Whatever the reason, the trees turned and twisted to create a barrier windbreak in the winter and provide a dense canopy of shade for the small herd of cows in the summer. Each fall, green bumpy-rinded fruit we called "horse apples" swayed heavily from the bois d'arc limbs, then dropped. Nothing grew underneath in the dense shade, the ground barren except for rotting horse apples and rounds of cow patties and swarms of flies.

A dug tank sat in one corner of the pasture, its earthen dam bulldozed strategically across a shallow draw. By summer the water level had receded and the dozen cows stood around knee-deep in chocolate-colored muck. Unidentifiable green stuff clung to their legs when they stumbled up and out onto dry ground.

In the evenings doves would fly in to water, making a skittish circle or two before lighting on top of the dam. The birds cocked their smooth heads from side to side, pecking at bits of gravel and stray seeds while they made their way down to the water's edge. I loved to watch those doves—their speed and grace, the iridescence of their heads—while I hid, stretched out in the tickle of needle grass, pretending I had a shotgun.

A scattering of native grasses and weeds covered the rest of the seventy acres—the needle grass I remember most, for true to its name it stuck and stung like hundreds of needles when it worked its way through my socks. But there were goat weeds, too, and yellow-blossomed bitterweeds and bull nettles. And over the years mesquite trees had spread across the land, brought up from Mexico and into Texas, so the old-timers said, by the droppings of steers on the long cattle drives north.

A prior owner of the seventy acres had made a misguided run at clearing the mesquite, and now second-growth shoots and sprouts had grown back from the stumps he had cut and turned the trees into thick bushes. A half-dozen shoots, some as big around as my skinny forearm, curved eight feet or more out and up from each stump.

Mesquite may not be all bad—some indigenous and hungry poor of this hemisphere are said to have ground the dried seeds into a flour of sorts—but around where we lived the trees were hated. Mesquite roots run deep—up to fifty feet—and suck the water away from the native grasses, and their thorns puncture even the heaviest of tractor tires. Cattle won't eat the foliage and the wood isn't fit for fence posts. "Worthless dadgum trees," Daddy called them.

11 / *Seven Days Working*

DADDY DROPPED ME off at the south end of the seventy acres that Monday with my tools and supplies—enough, I hoped, for the week. Besides the axe and file, I had a blanket to sleep on and a cardboard box of food—mostly cans of pork and beans and sardines and Vienna sausages, a giant jar of Peter Pan peanut butter, and a pint of my mother's plum jelly. There was a Crisco can of her crisp tea cakes, a couple of squishy bags of marshmallows and a package of powdered sugar doughnuts. Three or four loaves of Mrs. Baird's sandwich slices drooped across the top of it all. I had a box of kitchen matches and a roll of toilet paper, a stained hand towel and a broken-in half-bar of Ivory soap.

Ten gallons of water sloshed in a galvanized insulated can that Daddy tilted on its edge so that he could walk it over to the shade of the bois d'arc grove where I would make my camp.

Together, Daddy and I worked a fifty-gallon drum of diesel fuel out of the propped-up trunk of the car and let it slide out, landing with a thump on the black, cracked ground. I had a rusty pump-up sprayer fitted with a shoulder strap that I filled with diesel so I could douse the stumps as I went. I was to cut and spray—the only way we knew to kill the invasive mesquite—then stack and burn the tops, all the while trying not to impale a foot on a two-inch mesquite thorn.

Since the sprouts of second-growth mesquite grow out in thick bunches from the cut-over stumps, getting a clear swing with the axe wasn't easy. There was always the danger of the sharp blade glancing off a sprout and slicing your foot, or a mis-hit with the axe whipping a springy branch with its thorns across your face and catching an eye.

Daddy took the axe, motioned for me to follow him. He found

a mesquite bush to his liking and spread his feet wide, crouched low so that he could swing the axe under the profusion of spindly limbs. Daddy wore his farm clothes—khaki shirt, khaki pants and a scarred-up, worn-out pair of wing tip dress shoes. His shoulders were sloped, but strong. The backs of his hands were splotchy from too many years of working in the sun. He pulled a straw hat—a sweat-stained, discarded dress hat—tight over his brow, and attacked the tree. It didn't have a chance. With six or seven angry swings of the axe, Daddy was down to bare stump. He kicked the limbs into a pile of sorts and handed me the axe.

I took it uncertainly. Daddy pointed to the next mesquite tree, pulled his hat back, wiped his sleeve across his high forehead, across the thinness of his straight combed-back hair, and waited. I advanced on the tree, eyeing the curving spraddle of limbs, trying to position myself so that I could get a clean swing at the base of the sprouts. I spread my feet apart, bent low, and swung the axe. Hard. As hard as I could. As if the axe were a baseball bat. The axe blade hit a thick sprout straight on and bounced to the side. I could feel the vibration all through my body, but I managed to hang on to the axe.

"Dadgummit, Donnie," Daddy said. He took the axe, held it out. "You have to swing it at an angle. Not so hard. You can't beat a tree down; you have to cut it down." He swung the axe easily at a downward angle and the sprout fell to one side. He looked at me, the look a question. I nodded. "I need to get my gloves," I said. Daddy shook his head and followed me back to the shade of the bois d'arcs.

For a few minutes he lectured me on the dangers of working alone out on the seventy acres. Besides the likelihood that I would mangle my foot, there were copperheads and coral snakes lazing, curled in the mesquites' shade, and yellow jacket and red wasp nests hanging from their branches, and hornet and bumblebee nests secreted underground to be accidentally disturbed. Colonies of red ants rose like miniature pyramids across the land, with busy patterns of two-inch wide trails connecting them. Spiders of all sizes and colors stretched their webs from tree to tree and scorpions waited under rocks and dead limbs.

While Daddy talked I glanced at the sky where buzzards soared in long, looping circles above me, waiting, I figured, for me to make some last, fatal mistake.

Finally, and with obvious relief, Daddy said he would pick me up early next Sunday. He opened his car door and hesitated a minute. He looked at me, then out over the flatness of the seventy acres. I figured he would tell me to be careful, and I was ready to nonchalantly dismiss his concern.

"See how much you can get cleared," he said, with a wave of his hand. Skepticism in his voice, skepticism in his eyes. He slid into the car, hit the starter a couple of times before it caught.

"You know where the Jenkins' place is." He nodded to the west where I could just see the gray shingled top of a house. "You have a problem, Roy Clyde will give you a hand." He eased into the car, slammed the door shut. He tapped his pipe on the edge of the door. Ashes fell, drifted away. He filled the pipe once more from the flat can of Sir Walter Raleigh, punched the tobacco firm with his thumb. "Keep that axe sharp," he said.

I told him I would.

Daddy gripped the unlit pipe in his teeth and with a nod pulled away. I waited in the shade until the Ford was out of sight and the dust from the road drifted to the north.

I was alone. I turned and stared across the pasture, across the tops of the hundreds and hundreds of mesquite trees. An impossible job, I thought, and felt myself sink. There was no way I could even start to clear all of that mesquite.

I groped around in the grocery sack and found the peanut

butter and a butcher knife, located my mother's plum jelly. I split open the plastic on a loaf of bread with the point of the knife and smeared a sandwich thick. I found a spot without a fresh cow patty next to a tree and slumped to the ground. I leaned back against the smooth bark and ate. Flies lit on my sandwich while I chewed. I didn't even care.

When I finished, I wiped my mouth on my hand, wiped my hand on my jeans. A lizard worked its way down the tree and stopped just above my shoulder. The lizard bobbed its head, puffed out its orange throat, waiting for something. I was thirsty. I knew I should get to work, but I sat there and watched the lizard for a long time.

BY EVENING I HAD CUT what I considered a respectable amount of mesquite. I had started out to make one huge stack for a bonfire, but already had abandoned the one-stack method, discovering that dragging the thorny branches through the knee-high weeds got old in a hurry. So now—as I looked back from the shelter of the bois d'arc grove out across the long shadows of dusk—three mounds of scraggly mesquite loomed, hump-like growths on the flat land. Not bad, I thought. Not bad at all.

I made a small fire, opened a can of ranch-style beans three-quarters of the way around. I bent the tin lid back for a handle and eased the can into the edge of the fire. In a moment the label flared up in a quick blaze. Charred bits of paper swirled upwards in a smoky circle.

I devoured the beans straight from the can with a tin spoon and packed myself with a half-dozen slices of white bread and most of the Crisco can of the tea cakes.

The blanket didn't provide much padding, but the accumulation of bois d'arc leaves and crumbled cow patties made it a manageable bed.

The fire died down. The stars winked through the branches of the trees. A trio of cows came around. One sniffed at the toes of my socked feet, then jumped back when I wiggled them. Something stirred along the fence row at my back. I bolted upright, tense, straining to hear. But all I heard was the plop, plop, plop, of cow droppings and the swish of cow tails. I lay back down, somehow comforted by the closeness of the cows, the pungency of their smells. I reached out, found my axe and drew it next to me, both hands on the handle. I slept well.

Tuesday: Day Two

WORK WAS NOT UNFAMILIAR, for one of my earliest memories is straining to pull my Radio Flyer wagon down the sidewalk in front of our house when we lived in Houston. We occupied the upstairs half of a duplex on Colquitt Street in a modest neighborhood not that far from downtown. I went door to door collecting newspapers from our neighbors, stacking them into the wagon, and finally, with Daddy's help, pulling the overflowing wagon to the neighborhood fire station several blocks away. The newspapers somehow fit into the war effort, for this was 1944, the year before Daddy left his job at Standard Oil of Texas and moved us to Athens where he struck out on his own.

At Standard Oil Daddy was a scout, traveling around the eastern part of the state, keeping the company current as to oil plays here and there. An oil scout was the lowest white-collar job in the company, one rung down from a landman. Daddy was then in his mid-thirties, but without a college education, and realized that he couldn't compete in the company hierarchy.

At the end of the war Daddy quit Standard Oil and moved us to East Texas. There, around Athens, he had made some connections so that he could survive on "day work" as an independent oil man—working land titles in the courthouses around, then negotiating oil leases with the local landowners.

Later, as a teenager, I learned the trade, found that the mysteries of land titles with their web of mineral conveyances and reservations, their foreclosures and wills, opened before me as clearly as sentence diagrams. The logic of it all, the inevitable rational movement of generations of owners across and through a piece of land touched something basic, intuitive in me and by the time I was seventeen I ran titles in the Henderson County clerk's office and had bought my first oil lease on a town lot in Van, Texas. But that was later.

My parents found a generous-sized lot to build on near the south edge of Athens. The house they built was my mother's conception, a low-slung ranch style with a roof of white, crushed marble. Daddy enlisted the help of a couple of brothers-in-law and found a carpenter who had his own tools. In the aftermath of the war building materials were scarce or nonexistent, so Daddy and his helpers tore down a barn and an abandoned farmhouse out north of Kerens and hauled the lumber back east the thirty miles to Athens. Nails had to be pulled and rotten ends trimmed, but from here and there Daddy gathered most everything needed for a house.

As soon as the roof was on and the walls were up, we moved in. Daddy punched holes in a bucket and hung it from a limb of the oak tree behind the house. Mother heated water in a black wash pot on an open fire and filled the bucket for our make-do shower.

The first couple of years we had a Jersey cow that Mother milked early and late. We kept Bossy on a long rope, and several times a day she had to be moved from one grassy patch to the next in the unfenced field that stretched out behind our lot.

There was talk of a few chickens, or maybe guinea hens, which Mother favored, but Daddy balked at both. His mother and daddy still had long metal sheds out behind their house in Kerens crammed full of white leghorns. Egg gathering and chicken plucking made smelly, hard, monotonous work that had earned them nothing but worry.

Both Mother and Daddy were resourceful and hardworking, but torn between the old ways and the new. In the 1960s they would have been at home with the back-to-the-earth movement—minus the tie-dye, long hair, dope-smoking elements. For they were surely after self-sufficiency, possessed a dream that with enough land and enough cows, and a half-acre vegetable garden and some fruit trees they would be able to make it. They would pick wild berries and plums for jellies and preserves; Mother would can and freeze and scrimp and save and that would be enough. And the shadow of the Depression would never fall across Daddy's shoulders again. By gum!

Mother found the bricks for the house, had them trucked up from a demolition job in Palestine, a town south of Athens. A black man methodically cleaned the old mortar from the huge stack of bricks one at a time. For a cleaning device he nailed soda bottle caps upside down, edge to edge, row after row on a wide pine board, and scraped the bricks back and forth until the mortar crumbled away.

Mother instructed the local masons to set aside their chalk lines and lay the bricks in a random, drunken pattern—something she had evidently seen done in Houston. This must have been the most difficult task of all, for over the years her battle with the brickmasons was the house-building story most often repeated. Mother did tell stories—I guess she always had, for from childhood someone had tagged her Talkie, a nickname that stuck on Georgianne Baxter Watt until she died.

Snapshots of Mother made when the house was completed disclose an attractive woman in her early thirties. She is tall and slender, and appears to be confident. Her dark hair hangs loose to her shoulders. She is smiling, a little self-consciously it seems, into the camera. The black and white snapshot does not mirror the smoothness of her olive skin, but picks up the strong bone structure in her face. She looks happy.

Before Daddy got on with Standard Oil in Houston, he had worked as a permit man for a geophysical research company—GSI—and we traveled with a crew across much of Texas and Louisiana and Oklahoma (where I was born and lived the first two weeks of my life). We moved every two to six weeks, a hard life for Mother and her two babies, but it was a job, a good enough job, when work was still hard to come by at the tail end of the Depression.

When Mother had the chance to stop, she did with a vengeance, and would never move from that house they built in Athens. Mother and Daddy both grew up in Navarro County—around the little community of Bazette—just down the road from the seventy acres of mesquite where I worked, and Mother found it right to be near her kin. Her mother and daddy had lived near Bazette and Daddy's parents lived not far away, in Kerens. And the place was overflowing with sisters and brothers and in-laws and cousins too numerous to name. Athens was close, nearby, but far enough away so that Mother and Daddy could lead their lives somewhat independent of their families.

The house they built in Athens was solid enough, but the site for the house was in a swale of sorts, the land never built up, so they poured the foundation too low, and to this day heavy rains flood the back porch and spread across the kitchen floor.

The interior of the house was plain, with eight-foot ceilings and recycled pine floors—the kitchen counter topped with green linoleum, the cabinets white painted boards with cheap glass knobs. They tacked canvas to the walls and ceilings and covered every inch with wallpaper. Mother loved pink and she loved roses and the house reflected her taste. Doors were hard to come by or expensive—it was years later before we had a door on our bathroom. I remember one Christmas—I must have been ten or so—when Mother, anticipating a gathering of kin, thumb-tacked a hemmed sheet across the bathroom door opening to afford some privacy. It was some years later, after I had left home for college, that the bedroom I had shared with Dick, my younger brother, finally got a door.

By the time I was seven I mowed yards with our rotary-blade pushmower. One yard was too overgrown for me to handle—I will never forget finally giving up, the way Mr. Keeble grudgingly handed over a quarter for the little work I had accomplished.

The summer I was eleven I got a job spreading asphalt gravel with a long handled shovel out at the site of the soon-to-be Star View drive-in theater. I rode my bike the mile or so from our house out the Palestine highway every day for three weeks, and in the end earned a free pass for the rest of the summer to both of the movie houses on the square, the Dixie and the Liberty. I went most afternoons the rest of that summer, taking my four-year-old brother along. We sat through innumerable double features of Johnny Mack Brown and Lash Larue and Gene Autrey and Roy Rogers. Admission for a kid was nine cents. I never figured up, and didn't care, what I had earned in free movies at that job. I only remember the flicker of dark, magical afternoons lost in the adventures of the West, the way the world began to open before me in sepia-toned newscasts.

This was Texas, this place where we lived, but the West of the movies might as well have been on another planet. For East Texas is much more of the South than of the West. Farms here, ranches there. Rain here (in good years) and vacant miles of sand there. Truck farmers here, ranchers there. A visible minority of blacks here, a not-so-visible minority of Hispanics there. This was the South, simply put. Maybe an extension of sorts—an overlay that produced a mutant hybrid, perhaps. But it was the Bible-thumping, God-fearing, whiskey-sneaking, good-old-boy-run rural South, with ample portions of generosity and kindness and patriotism thrown in. No better and no worse than most other parts of the country in the 1950's, and not a bad place for a boy to grow up.

THE SUMMER I WAS THIRTEEN, I moved up to mowing pastures, riding Daddy's battered Ford tractor, pulling behind a mower made from the rear axle of a Mack truck. The mower's velocity was geared to the tractor's speed. The tractor slowed, the blades on the big mower slowed. The tractor stopped, the blades stopped—so it was imperative to keep the tractor moving—and I bounced across the pastures and churned up little inclines and slid through turns while the engine roared and whined.

Daddy bought the tractor—used if you were selling, "wore-out" if you were buying—from a black mortician by the name of Preacher Brown, who ran his business out of a square brick building out on Highway 31. I went along to witness the negotiations, Daddy hoping to teach me something of the fine art of trading.

I turned out a liability to the procedure, I'm sure, unable to hide my disappointment every time Daddy began to walk away from Preacher Brown, shaking his head in mock disbelief over the man's pride in the tractor. For I saw the Ford tractor as a way to get some wheels under me, even if it would be across hard-rut fields.

In spite of my presence, Daddy finally made the deal. I drove the tractor eight miles north to the Texas Stream, a tract of land Daddy had bought and named the year before. While he checked me out on the gears and the brakes and cautioned me about flipping the tractor on a slope (Mother had lost a nephew in just that way), he commented on the now-consummated trade. "More deals are lost by saying too much than by saying too little." Daddy knew when to speak, when to remain quiet. Not a bad trait at all.

Mowing carried with it a certain pleasure. The swish, swish, swish of the heavy blades snapping through the tough weeds, the spray of grasshoppers scattering before me, the field mice and rats and rabbits all finding cover in the ever-diminishing circle that the mower made—until finally, just before I made the last, weed-shredding pass at full throttle, the rodents and rabbits and insects all scurried out of the remaining band of weeds, frantically leaping and flying and hopping for shelter.

Daddy would come out to the pasture at the end of the day. While I chugged ice water in the shade of a tree, he'd study my day's work. He'd stand with his arms folded, his pipe clenched tight in his teeth. Every once in a while he'd wander out into the field to pull an uncut, bowed-over goat weed that a tractor wheel had laid flat. Then he'd stand at that spot for a few minutes before he gave a little nod and moved back towards the car.

I never got a "Nice job, son," no praise of any kind. Not for hard work, not for good work—hard and good being the baseline, the minimum required level of accomplishment, and for sure nothing to go on about.

I took off two weeks from mowing that summer to run the Red Top Store, Dee Tyner's little grocery store down the Cayuga highway a half mile or so from our house. Dee Tyner had grown up with Daddy in Navarro County, around what was then the community of Bazette. He and Daddy weren't exactly friends, for they never saw each other outside of the Red Top Store or church, but they were cronies, and bantered good-naturedly when Daddy made a tobacco run to the store.

I guess Dee Tyner and Daddy had talked it over, because somehow, for two weeks while Mr. Tyner and his round wife and four boys vacationed, I opened the store every morning at seven and locked it tight at seven every evening. This paid real money—the only reason I got time off from mowing pastures.

At thirteen, for the first time, I faced adult temptation. For those two weeks I stood behind the store's checkout counter, in charge of rows of Baby Ruths and Butterfingers and Hershey bars. There were forbidden squares and pouches of chewing tobacco, round tins of snuff, and cigarettes. The freezer bulged with fudge bars and Eskimo Pies and Dixie Cups with movie stars' pictures on the under side of each lid. And all of those dollar bills in the cash register.

I did sneak a candy bar or two and chewed some Dubble Bubble on the house; I bit a small corner off a square of hard-pressed Day's Work chewing tobacco, worked it back to the corner of my jaw where I thought it belonged and nearly burned a hole in my cheek. I chased it by chugging a free Grapette. Otherwise, I ran a straight-arrow store.

By nature I am not particularly honorable nor honest, beset by and victim to most imagined temptations. I would hope that I fall not too far afield on the bell curve of decency, but from early on any tendencies I had towards flimflam fell easy victim to that old bugaboo, guilt.

That summer when I reigned over the Red Top Store and all its contents, the God who ruled over the South Palestine Street Church of Christ was metamorphosing for me, becoming more complex while I was growing suspicious of His existence. But He still held a ferocity that kept me, for the most part, in line. That weird mixture of God and guilt and church kept me from sneaking a strawberry ice cream pie from the freezer and devouring it in the store room. I coveted that pie, its silky pinkness, the swirl of strawberry jam and whipped cream on the top. I hid it in a corner of the freezer underneath some popsicle boxes so no customer could find it. It stayed there the entire two weeks I ran the store. Now, I wish I had eaten it.

Being on my own for the first time—with real, grown-up responsibility—instilled (or reinforced) an incipient independence that would never leave me. I liked being in charge, being alone for the most part, for there were no more than a couple of dozen customers who stopped by the store on most days, and most of them between four and six. To this day, I find a certain thrill sweep over me when I take off on some adventure alone, whether it is the start of an essay or a novel, or tooling in my pickup down that well-worn path that crosses the Rio Grande and leads to the freedom of Mexico.

BEING ALONE ON THE LAND, cutting mesquite, was an adventure too. Here my mind roamed horizon to horizon with nothing to harness it. When nothing in particular is in focus, them suddenly everything matters the same. There were no profundities—I was no young Stephen Hawking—but I did have a natural curiosity about what I would later know as cosmology.

This mostly involved resting after ferociously hacking down a stretch of mesquite trees, lying back in a prickly bed of needle grass and staring at the sky. I tried somehow to imagine myself beyond the clouds, then beyond the faint ghost of a daytime moon, finally propelling myself into the vastness beyond until dizzy, I would shudder and throw back my hands to grasp wads of grass to keep from falling off the face of the earth.

A pickup eased down the dirt road next to the seventy acres a couple of times that second day, breaking my reverie. When I heard it coming I turned into a working maniac, chopping mesquite like a madman, hoping that whoever cruised by would be impressed and word would somehow get back to Daddy. The pickup slowed a little and a man gave me a wave. It was Roy Clyde Jenkins, I figured, who lived on the farm down the way. Some days his wife would be a shadow riding with him, stiff and straight on the passenger side. I always waved back, always hoped he wouldn't stop.

By the end of that second day I had got the hang of it, and could see a sizable indentation in the wall of mesquite. A half-dozen head-high stacks dotted the land. Already my arms held a patchwork of scratches and scrapes, and once a limb sprang across my face drawing a thin line of blood.

I carried an Army surplus canteen of water as I worked. I had bought this canteen a couple of years before when I turned twelve, old enough to join the Boy Scouts. This troop, the only one in Athens, was sponsored by the First Methodist Church, and it took some powerful talking to convince Mother that I wouldn't somehow become a Methodist by hanging around in the church's basement on Thursday nights.

Scouting was a big investment, and took a trip down to Penney's to purchase the uniform, and then out on the Tyler highway to the Army/Navy surplus store to get all the paramilitary paraphernalia that scouting required.

I have a tendency to quit—for whatever reasons—a by-now long history of not sticking things out when the going gets tough. Or routine. Or boring. Certain organized things bother me—often through no fault but my own, I admit. I dropped out of kindergarten half way through that first year of structured learning, bored and jaded with school already. The next year, as a first grader, I made it through a month or so of twice-a-week piano lessons before the temptations of after-school games of chase and tops and marbles won out.

Much later, as a freshman at TCU, I joined the Air Force ROTC since all of the other basketball players had joined, and quit three days later when some gung-ho cadet told me that the pin with wings had to be fastened to my collar exactly one-quarter inch from its edge.

But quitting the Boy Scouts was a different story, I like to think. The weekly meetings consisted of our leader, A.C. Rogers, driving up in his Tom's Toasted Peanuts delivery truck and gathering us into that small basement room of the Methodist church. A.C. was—there's no polite way to put it—fat. His gut hung over his belt and he could barely pull himself up into his step-van truck.

A.C.'s first order of business in the privacy of that overheated little room was a dirty joke of some sort, followed by a belch or a loud fart or both. Then it was outside where all of us boys were instructed to take off our puke-green Boy Scout belts and form a belt line, six or seven of us on each side, making an alley-way of sorts. Then each of us had to walk—not run—through that line while the others flayed our butts with the belts. Buckles could not be used; this concession kept the whole ordeal just above Nazi Youth Camp brutality. The belt line would make men of us, A.C. preached, and I suppose he believed it.

After a few months I somehow earned my Tenderfoot badge and promptly quit. This canteen was the only good that came from that experience, and it had a leak that my Uncle Frank had to solder for me. On the seventy acres I carried the canteen slung by its strap over my shoulder. After hacking down three or four trees, I would stop, take a drink of the warm water while kneeling in the shade of a mesquite. During this rest time I sank my axe into one of the newly cut stumps and filed the blades until they shined silver and smooth. I learned to take pride in this skill, thought Daddy would approve the finesse I had developed with axe and file.

I moved on, just a few steps between trees, and tossed my canteen to the side. I set myself again, my feet spread wide, my gloves, already worn and supple, tightly gripping the handle of the axe. I swung, slicing a low shoot at the outer edge of a tree. With that swing, to my horror, I sliced off the hind leg of a rabbit.

The rabbit was small, would have fit into the flat of both my hands. It must have been hiding in the thick shelter of the mesquite sprawl. Now the poor animal lay on its side, one eye staring up at me. It didn't even struggle.

"Shit," I said—shit being a word I thought often, but spoke out loud only safely with my friends or when alone. I wish I could say that I felt bad—which I did—and as an act of mercy put the poor rabbit out of its misery, rescued it from a fate of dying of thirst or in the claws of a hawk or the jaws of a fox. But I couldn't bring myself to do it. I slung the axe into the mesquite in anger and disgust. I made my way back to the bois d'arc grove and the late afternoon shade.

I eased down at the base of a tree and leaned back holding a mason jar of water. Then I cried. I now think those were angry tears. I hated this job. The heat, the day-after-day of peanut butter sandwiches. The ants and the flies and the smell of diesel fuel that I couldn't wash off my hands. Why had my mother let Daddy leave me out here alone, working at a man's job? And what kind of man would even work this way? A hobo wouldn't live like this. Why couldn't I still be playing ball or fishing the way I had when I was eleven or twelve, the way other boys my age were doing? And now I was a rabbit maimer, to boot.

It would have been easier if I had cut my own foot with the axe. For a few moments I wished I had. I closed my eyes and could see it clearly—the shiny blade slicing through my tennis shoe, blood spurting everywhere, but me, being resourceful and brave, wrapping my leather belt tightly around my calf to stop the flow of blood, then hobbling the two miles to Roy Clyde's house, using the axe for a cane. There Mrs. Jenkins would call my mother to come for me. I had learned, way earlier than this, how Mother responded to bad news, the way her save-and-sacrifice part clicked in for emergencies. Even years later, calling her long distance, I could hear Mother's breath quicken when I relayed some problem back to her. One of my kids in trouble, a little health flare-up, working too hard—it didn't matter—she was ready for the rescue. But start in telling her how terrific things were going, how well everyone was, and you'd end up with a dial tone in your ear. While I waited, Mrs. Jenkins would prop me up on her worn-out sofa and bring me a couple of biscuits left over from breakfast with some blackberry jam and a tall, blue glass of cold milk. On the drive back home my mother would scold Daddy, and I would never have to work again.

I stayed in the shade of the bois d'arc grove until the sun dropped below the tops of the mesquite, then made my way to the tank where I lay in the grass and stared at the sky until a huge owl swept low and silent over the water.

Wednesday: Day 3

THE NEXT MORNING I eased out into the mesquite with my breakfast—a peanut butter and jelly sandwich—in hand. I toted the sprayer, heavy with diesel fuel, strapped over one shoulder, and my canteen of water slung over the other. It was early, the sun just up. The grass, wet with dew, sparkled like a field of frost. I hated it; after only a few steps my tennis shoes and socks had soaked through.

I located the last tree I had cut the afternoon before, and finally found my axe where I had slung it, but the rabbit was gone. I hoped that it might have hopped off three-legged somehow, for I had seen a dog limping around a welding shop in town that managed quite well with a missing leg. I consoled myself with the idea that rabbits don't have much of a life span anyway, and got back to work, afraid that Daddy would somehow be able to tell that I had stopped cutting mesquite early the day before.

I figured I could cut and stack a mesquite tree in twenty minutes or so. On the average there must be about eight shoots sprouting up from each tree stump, and it took a dozen swings of the axe to sever them all. I had to cut some of them twice, once wherever my axe happened to hit, and then again to get the shoots cut down low, right at the stump, my axe more often than not dulling itself in the dark, rock-pitted ground.

I pumped the sprayer to build up the pressure, locked the handle in place, and shot streams of diesel fuel on the stumps of the severed sprouts until they gleamed, oily in the sun.

Then I dragged the tangle of mesquite growth away and pitched it as best I could onto a new, rising pile of brush. For a few moments I knelt in the shade of the next tree while I gulped water from my canteen. Every few trees I stopped to sharpen my axe, file smooth a blade that I'd dinged and dulled. Cutting mesquite was no big deal now. Twenty minutes a tree. I was moving on. I stopped to calculate. That's three trees an hour, say twenty-five to thirty trees a day cut and stacked, the stumps sprayed with diesel fuel. Not bad.

I stood tall and gazed to the north across the spread of tree tops, suddenly worried. Seventy acres, I thought, less the narrow lane that runs the length of the place on the east side, less a half acre for the tank and the open ground around it. Then there's the little shed and the make-shift wire corral, another half-acre or so. A clearing here and there around the fence lines. I rounded off the acres of mesquite to sixty-six. SIXTY-SIX!

Shit, I thought. Thirty trees to the acre, I figured, thirty trees a day, outside. An acre a day. That's sixty- six days. There are twenty-two work days a month, on average. That's three months. My entire summer cutting mesquite. Shit! I moaned the wonderfully expressive word out loud this time, and then I yelled it out. SHIT! Across the way a buzzard lifted off a crooked fence post in alarm, flapped its way up and around in a tight circle, then settled on the same fence post again, unperturbed.

This was the summer I was to get my hardship driving license and spend nights circling the Dairy Queen in Daddy's Ford with my pals—Stick and Satch and Jugbutt, and all the rest—looking for action, acting tough around the junior college guys who hung out there and made moves on the local girls. Our girls.

My sister Sally didn't have to work, and she was three years older. Girls had it made. It wasn't fair. But thinking it not being fair was as far as it went in our family. I would never complain to Daddy, for complaining wasn't tolerated. Mother might have been more sympathetic, but I didn't want her to think I was a crybaby. And Sally. Well, we grew up not really talking. She would be a senior in Athens High this coming year, while I was a freshman. She was smart, studied a lot, played the piano, and had her own friends.

It's a shame Sally and I weren't allies growing up, there in the same house, her bedroom at the opposite end of the hall from the bedroom I shared with my seven-year-old brother. Somehow we were never close, and for a long time I thought it was just that boy/girl dichotomy, with me interested in basketball and baseball and football, while Sally studied and practiced piano and slept over at girlfriends' slumber parties.

But it was more than that. We grew up in a house of distrust, of judgment, a house imbued with the fear of failing, falling short of expectations that were never openly listed, but were implicit in body language, in the unspoken, but implied rules. This was a house where intimacy might be withheld as punishment, where Church of Christ fundamentalism was translated into, and confused with, social and familial responsibilities and requirements.

Daddy might yell at me when I couldn't cut off a half-wild cow that bolted from the corral, or when I let a yearling struggle out of my grip while he tried to inject a syringe of something into its neck, or when I let the tractor's leaky radiator overheat because I daydreamed while mowing the pasture instead of noticing the steam rising in front of me.

But it was Mother who controlled things, carefully allotting her affection and approval, never—hardly ever—raising her voice. Cutting her eyes around with an icy stare, turning away, leaving you standing alone in a room when she didn't agree or didn't approve. Shaking her head in disappointment.

Although I carried the imagination of a writer, I believe, most of my life, the act of writing, the putting down of words on paper, came late for me—my first story, an anemic four pages, secretly written when I was forty-six, a novel and book of short stories both published in my fifty-fourth year. The subject of writing or publishing in my mother's house in those years sent her quickly retreating from my presence. Was she embarrassed, ashamed, or simply lacking a context to discuss this new passion I had? I never knew. So I mostly kept quiet. It was as if I had brought a new lover home for Mother to meet, introduced to her a Las Vegas showgirl or a black woman, or even a Yankee—God forbid!

In my late thirties, a year or so after the nasty end of a disastrous first marriage, I did bring my new bride-to-be home to meet my parents. She was a lovely woman, gracious, attractive, full of life, but not a Southerner, and she worked hard for the rest of my mother's life to win acceptance. On that first day at my parents' house, Mother took me aside to ask if my fiancée was just a divorcee—which she was—or a widow. Mother's shoulders fell when I disclosed the truth. She turned quickly away. Adultery is what I had committed, I knew, Biblical adultery, anyway, and the New Testament passages so ready on my mother's tongue telegraphed through my head.

The last conversation I had with my mother was by telephone, just a couple of weeks before her fatal heart attack, and her last words to me before I mumbled a good-bye and hung up were about my collection of short stories, a book that had won a prize and been well-received, even praised in reviews, including one in *The Dallas Morning News*, the only newspaper that mother trusted, the only one she ever read. "Now I know there are people who are like that," she said. "But I wish you hadn't written that third story in your book..."—a story of brotherly conflict and betrayal and love.

You should be ashamed, I felt her say, and shamed I was, but not in the way she meant.

Sally and Dick and I should have conspired to keep our sanity through all of this, or maybe it didn't register on them, for to this day, my mother dead for more than three years, Dick will proclaim that Mother was an angel, a perfect mother, and Sally gets all teary, somehow nostalgic for a childhood and a mother I never knew.

Why does this happen? We all grew up in the same house, in the fifties, a harmless decade for the most part—at least in Athens, Texas. But harm was done somehow, and three children became adults whose lives, at times, have been out of kilter.

But let me speak only for myself. My first memory is the taste of my own shit. I know it, I can still taste it. Psychologists maintain that we have no conscious memory before the age of two or three; they would insist that this distasteful, repugnant memory of mine is layered and distorted by subsequent events, that a good bout of psychotherapy would get to the root of this.

Well, I say: Smell my fingers. Listen to my story.

I'm standing in my baby bed, holding on to the side rail, balancing myself with one hand, holding my other shit-smeared hand out towards my mother. My yellow excrement is thick between my fingers, smeared across my mouth. The rich, fecund smell fills my head, my memory. My reaching out to Mother is a plea, an acknowledgment to her that this is not right, that I have done something wrong.

How did I know this, still a baby? Perhaps it is her anger at me, even though I am only a year or so old, her anger that tells me I am bad, that this is wrong, that I am a shameful thing. Because, as a one-year-old, I have no sense of myself as baby or as boy or as male being. But only as a shameful, shit-eating thing, in that instant filled with guilt and remorse and a deep chasm of shame that I will carry the rest of my life.

Until now, including this very instant of now, when I pause while typing these words and without thinking chew on the ragged edge of skin around one fingernail—when that taste, the smell and taste of my own bodily waste, and the anger of my mother all fill me, hang in my nostrils, hide deep in the secret, mysterious windings of my brain, always there.

I must have cried at the time, cried out my discomfort, knowing something had gone wrong, knowing somehow that the taste and smell and stickiness shouldn't be a part of my life. I cried out. And Mother came to me. With anger.

And who could blame her? A moment before she came I was distressed, but innocent. She was annoyed, perhaps, but well-intentioned. I pulled myself up, crying, my hand extended and between us my shame somehow was created.

Along with my anger. The axe this morning is brutal in my hands, the mesquite falling to this side and that side, and the brush piles grow higher. I won't stop even to eat, I think, I'll clear the whole shitty pasture this week. I'll show them. Daddy will be amazed and Mother will tell me what a fine son I am. I swing the axe harder and harder, move from clump to clump of mesquite. Already my T-shirt hangs wet on my back. I stop to wipe the sweat that blurs my eyes, but it is not sweat, it is tears.

We all have divides in our lives, times when the flow of events and emotions and needs and disappointments seem to narrow to a trickle, before suddenly flowing once again in a rush, possibly in a new direction. Changes that seem gradual, incremental at the time, but in the course of a relatively long life, these events become markers, points from which you reorient your life. These watershed times shape the flow of your life. Swinging an angry axe must help you remember. Just six months earlier, a couple of days before Christmas, our family drove over to Kerens, the small town only six or seven miles south of this pasture where I cut mesquite. One of my mother's brothers and his wife had invited us to dinner at their modest frame house on a corner lot in town. My aunt served chicken spaghetti, I remember, for that ordinary casserole was something new, a dish I had never tasted. And my taste, my memory for tastes—you know by now—is acute.

My aunt and uncle had three sons, and after dinner, Kenneth Wayne—the youngest boy, who was seventeen years old—took me out on the town for a spin in his Model A.

We cruised the main street, up and down, back and forth, all four brick-paved blocks of it, each time circling around and through the giant legs of a Santa Claus that somehow the town's leaders had managed to erect where Main Street dead ends at the high school. (In another year this Santa would be transplanted to Dallas and become Big Tex, the symbol of the State Fair of Texas.)

The night was cold and clear. Kenneth Wayne stopped for a couple of his buddies who were hanging out, shivering on a downtown corner. They clambered into the back seat, full of talk, loud with solid country cussing, then worked an eight-foot two-by-four pine plank into the car with us, resting one end of it on my shoulder where I sat in the front seat.

Kenneth Wayne started the Model A back up and we headed south out of town. He turned towards me and grinned, a sly half-grin. "You ever been nigger knockin'?" he asked. The boys in the back hooted and hollered and one of them punched me in the shoulder. I shook my head. No.

We crossed the railroad tracks and the gravel road narrowed.

Kenneth Wayne slowed the car a little and the boys in the back leaned forward to see better. The object, I soon gathered, was to spot a "nigger" walking home at the edge of the road in the dark. The driver then maneuvered the car alongside the walker as close as he could. The boys in the back would extend the two-by-four as far out the open window as possible while bracing it against the back of the seat. The object was to knock a black man down. "Nigger knockin'" is brutal sport. I knew that at the time. I knew it was wrong, but I couldn't back out. Not then.

The only two men we passed that night moved well off the road before we roared by. They leapt across the muddy bar ditch and stood there, crouching, still and silent until we had raced past. The boys in the back stuck the two-by-four out the window anyway, as far as they could reach, and yelled, cussing and laughing.

Watershed times.

On the one hand there is this: a sense of community and family; a holiday dinner with our kin. On the other hand, there is degradation and cruelty, hate and fear disguised as brutal sport. Killing deer (which I have never done) and shooting doves (which I have) seem to be done with the same relish, spring from the same foul need to dominate and destroy that my cousin and his friends manifested when they took me "nigger knockin'" that cold December night.

Watershed times. Yes, on the one hand there is this way, and on the other hand there is that way. Times of choice, but we don't seem to make the choices ourselves. Mysteriously, they are made for us.

You taste your own shit and live in shame; you walk away from a rabbit you mortally wound; you cringe at brutal, racial "sport," but don't speak out, don't walk away.

In the arc of life a few critical events, measured only in moments, set off by parentheses, nudge us this way or that and we can never turn back.

Thursday: Day 4

I ENJOY MINDLESS WORK like this. Work that is physical, that becomes routine. Occasionally I say out loud, "Don't cut your foot off, dummy," when I mis-hit a mesquite sprout and the axe glances away. Cutting mesquite is not like mowing pastures, when all you have to do is align the tractor wheels to cut as wide a swath as possible each time you go around. Sure, you watch out for low-hanging limbs and hidden ravines that could flip you over. You glance at the fuel gauge and check the engine temperature, but mostly your mind is free to wander where it wants to go.

Working with an axe doesn't allow that kind of reverie, but there is a rhythm you fall into and still plenty of time for adolescent introspection. I spend Thursday trying to figure out sex.

Scaramouche, or rather, Eleanor Parker, the co-star of that movie, has captured my imagination. First—on the "Now Showing" poster framed outside the Dixie Theater—Eleanor Parker is spotlighted in glamorous full color in a low-cut, red dress. She is turned sideways, her long auburn hair falling, cascading seductively, almost hiding one blue eye. The tops of her breasts strain up, voluptuously ballooning, her skin is unspeakably smooth, and her look—directly at me—is inviting, beckoning, teasing. I can almost see (a truth later verified in the movie) her breasts rise and fall, rise and fall, with each rise the globes threatening to pop out of her red dress completely.

And Stewart Granger there behind her, handsome, decked out in a frilly cuffed shirt, tight trousers and boots, his hat at a rakish angle, ready to leap and slash and swirl in an interminably energetic sword fight, finally running his blade through some evil Count to win the favors of Eleanor Parker. The luckiest man in the world I figure then. Maybe I still do.

Today Scaramouche would be firmly stuck in the G category, well below the minimum titillation or violence required for a PG rating, but the movie stands as proof of the power of a fourteen-year-old's imagination. I lusted after Eleanor Parker, mentally groped as best I could for her even in my sleep, waking up to erections that took forever to subside.

Sally had a *Photoplay* magazine that somehow she openly kept in her bedroom. I still can't believe Mother knowingly permitted her to have it. Or maybe Mother harbored hidden dreams of her own that I never could have guessed. Anyway, whenever Sally was gone I flipped through the slick pages to my favorite photo, a full-body shot of Marilyn Monroe in a green, mesh bikini. The top, if you looked as close as you could, barely hid the auroral flesh of her nipples. I swear I could see her nipples.

Breasts were awfully important. In my real life—at school—I had my first strange encounter with breasts in the library. At noon, after lunch, I routinely wandered through the library, checking the table in the middle of the room that held the few new books that Mrs. Vermillion had ordered for that school year. I would skim through *The Tontine* or *The High and Mighty,* standing there, waiting, trying to concentrate while my breathing became shallow and rapid, my mouth dry with glorious anticipation.

In a few minutes Diedre Holt would edge up next to me, and pretend to be interested in what books I had discovered. Diedre was a pretty girl with long black hair and silky skin. She was petite, a little skinny at fourteen, I guess. But in the past few months she had budded quite remarkably in the breast category. As we made small talk, ostensibly concentrating on those fascinating books, Diedre would push a breast—oh lovely breast—padded though it might be, into my arm. She kept it there and I dared not move. But she did. Up and down my arm the little breast traveled, back and forth, until we were both frothed up to some degree, Diedre flushed and me with a genuine boner. We were always saved by the bell, Diedre hurrying off to her locker, while I waited for the library to clear out so I could slip out sideways, my back turned to Mrs. Vermillion.

This went on for some weeks, an unacknowledged ritual between us. I was too shy to ask her for a date, and somewhat confused (if not terrified) by her aggressiveness. Later that semester she started dating Ronnie Wilson, freshman quarterback phenom, and our rendezvous ended.

In January, Mrs. Vermillion asked me to be president of the Library Club—a reward for my conspicuous presence in the library the past semester—an honor I modestly accepted.

While I work I move back in time—a night two years ago. Ronnie Wilson and I are camping out in the pasture behind his house. The stars are thick waves of light against the night sky. Ronnie and I are in the same grade in school, but at that time he is thirteen, almost a year older, and has an older brother. Ronnie has already driven his brother's motorcycle, and his mother lets him drive the family Oldsmobile 88 before he even has a driver's license. Ronnie is worldly, my guide down the tricky, profane trail of life.

That night we lie there side by side and Ronnie starts talking about girls. Talking about women. I mostly listen. And my mind swirls and expands like the sky above me. Ronnie has an older cousin, a real woman, I thought back then, maybe seventeen or eighteen. She would—Ronnie told me, his voice quiet and low—lock her legs together, entwine them as tight as she could and tell Ronnie that he could touch her "there" if he was able to force her legs apart. He never could.

"Boy," I said, "I would give anything to have a cousin like that." I tried to imagine touching a woman "there," but my mind could barely imagine its way into that forbidden valley.

My cousin Cheryl was only a year or so older than me and skinny. I had hardly ever thought of her even having the potential of becoming a real woman, much less playing some kind of teasing game with me. I had other cousins, lots of them, but Cheryl and I grew up close, always playing together when her family lit back around Athens for a few months. Slats, her daddy, who was my mother's younger brother, worked oil fields, mostly out in West Texas where the Permian Basin had heated up. In between roughneck jobs, Slats and his wife Maxine, with Cheryl and her two baby brothers, would end up in Athens for short spells, and Cheryl and I spent a lot of play time together.

One winter day, it must have been a Saturday—for I was ten or eleven and not in school—I spent the day playing at Cheryl's house, a sparsely furnished garage apartment in a rundown area not many blocks north of the courthouse square. We played cards, mostly Fish and Old Maid, while Maxine berated my Uncle Slats in her god-awful snarl of a voice until he grabbed his jacket and slipped away.

Just before noon Maxine stormed into the room where Cheryl and I sat at the kitchen table dealing cards. She shoved her two bundled-up, runny-nosed toddlers towards the door and pulled her felt hat down to her ears. "I've had it," she announced. "I'm going shopping, over to Tyler. There's nothing worth having in this sorry town."

Cheryl set in to whining then, complaining to her mama that we were hungry and that we were bored and there was nothing to play with.

In disgust Maxine stomped to the refrigerator and found a half package of wieners that she slid across the yellow-topped dinette. Then she hurried to her bedroom and Cheryl and I got quiet. In a minute Maxine bristled back into the room. As she hot-stepped it to the door, she tossed us a couple of packages of rubbers. "Play with these," she said. "Balloons. That's all they're good for, anyway." She grabbed up her two boys, one in each arm. With her foot, she slammed the door behind her. The apartment shook as she stomped down the outside stairs.

Cheryl and I ate cold wieners for lunch. We blew up the "balloons" and played with them until we got bored again. I can't remember if Cheryl told me they were rubbers—she was older, had lived in lots of places—but I knew that the rubbers weren't really toys to be played with, that they were illicit, forbidden. Although the exact purpose stayed beyond me.

Slats died a couple of years later, fell over working a small field of tomatoes he had planted in a field out west of town. He was only forty when his heart gave out. I want to believe that Slats passed on with some relief, an overriding sense of his final escape.

The sex reverie business tended to frustrate me. So far, all of my fantasies had stayed only that, and I couldn't quite imagine how to push this sex thing further. Then the answer came to me. I needed a car. At least a driver's license and the use of our family's 1950 Ford sedan.

I attacked the mesquite with new energy, my mind traveling

to strange places deep down wooded lanes with only the glow from the car radio to light the way. On a good night you could pick up a blues station beamed out of Nashville, music that moaned and complained and celebrated the mysterious entanglements that awaited men and women. In spite of the misery of the blues—with its despair and anger and disappointments—what stayed with me was the promise of getting that magic right. Not forever, if the blues told the story true. But maybe for some few minutes on one dark night I might discover that magic, slid down low in the front seat of my daddy's Ford.

Friday: Day 5

I WOKE UP AGITATED, tired of the isolation, staying here alone, and sore from the work, from sleeping on the ground. My sun-reddened arms were crosshatched with scratches. The food was tasteless—breakfast, the stale last three of a package of powdered sugar donuts followed by a handful of marshmallows.

Now—for the most part—I was down to the basics: cans of pork and beans, cans of Vienna sausage, cans of sardines, all steaming in their tin cans. The dregs of the peanut butter and a little plum jelly I figured to save for tomorrow, my last full day.

After the first night or two, I'd been content to do without the light of a fire, too weary to build one—content, more or less, with the sky as seen from the darkened pasture. The heat during the day was not so bad, for there had been gusts of breeze and my T-shirt always hung heavy with sweat. Nights, though, the wind died and the heat fell slowly, still radiating from the ground around me hours after dark.

Today a dust devil whipped around me. It came from the field to the west of where I worked. I stopped to watch as dried grass and leaves and sand whirled and churned, the debris rising in a funnel thirty or forty feet high. The dust devil danced through the barbed wire fence, darted to the left and right. The effect was hypnotic. I didn't move, even when I could tell it was headed towards me.

The funnel was strangely, eerily silent—all of that motion and churning energy—yet I could hear only the rush of wind as it approached.

When the edge of the dust devil touched me with its cut and sting, I knelt with my head down, one arm up to protect my face. In a moment it was gone, not only moved on beyond me, but gone altogether, as if my presence in its eye had stolen its bluster and dissipated it into the heat of the summer air.

This left me with a tremendous sense of power. For the rest of the morning it energized me, filled me (I imagined) with the dust devil's power, as if I had stolen it. I felt supernaturally touched, taking this incident as a sign as powerful as the burning bush of the Bible.

The energy I felt wasn't directed towards the work, the cutting and spraying and stacking. It pulled at me, left me vaguely agitated and restless with a feeling that I should be somewhere else, doing something else I couldn't define.

But there was no other place I wanted to be. Home would be okay for supper and a shower, but after that I would be as stuck there as I was here.

I dreamed that having my own wheels would help, enable me to take off whenever I wanted, in any direction. But then I worried that I carried that trapped feeling inside of me. Maybe it would always be there.

Now a dilemma. In the next logical tree to cut, a pair of mourning doves had made their nest. When I moved near they flitted in and out, hopping on limbs back and forth. One of them, the female I think, made a big show of bursting out of the nest and hitting the ground some feet away, then struggling forward a few yards, fussing all the time. She was feigning injury, I knew, for I'd seen this before—a mother's instinct to draw me away from her young.

For the time being I worked around the tree, changed the arc of my clearing. If the bird nest tree stood out too much, I would have to be back.

Soon I fell easily into my pattern of cutting and spraying, dragging and stacking; my mind wandered with the rhythm of it all. I reached for the answer for my restlessness, for its roots.

From the time I was born in Shawnee, Oklahoma, in 1940, until our family came to rest in Athens four years later, we stayed on the move. Two weeks in Shawnee. Then briefly somewhere around Dallas. And—in no particular order—on to South Texas, with short stops in Falfurrias and Refugio. Then Palacios and Kemah along the Texas coast, staying a few weeks in worn-out, rundown houses, and rooms in houses, and by-the-week tourist cabins across southeast Texas and into Louisiana, from Shreveport on the north to the Cajun country of the south, and, finally, venturing as far east as Vicksburg, Mississippi.

My mother told these stories of our itinerant years more than a few times—years of packing and unpacking, of scrubbing out rust-stained commodes and four-legged bathtubs with boxes of Bon Ami, of airing out worn-thin mattresses and painting over grease-thick kitchen walls. Telling stories for her was easy, telling them only once seemingly impossible. Mother told these stories not with anger or resentment, but with a pride of sorts, an astonishment at having survived those times.

Daddy had a job, a good one for those post-Depression years, when steady work for a small weekly check was hard to come by.

From 1940 to 1943 our family—my older sister, Sally, my mother and Daddy, and me, just a baby—traveled with a crew, fifteen or so men who shot seismographic lines across the would-be oil fields of that part of the country. They were gypsies in a way, although modestly paid, caravaning the big trucks and pickups that belonged to Geophysical Services Inc. from place to place. Their wives and kids rag-tagged along behind, or often hurried ahead to claim homes as best they could from what few places were available for short-term rent in those backwater towns.

Maybe all that moving—the constant motion of those wheels turning, of waking up in different rooms with different sounds and different angles of light and different smells—set in motion some need for change that attached itself to my DNA, so that movement and change and the grit of my own self all became rolled up into one slick-treaded tire, always rolling.

When we settled into that house in Athens, Daddy still traveled, taking day trips to nearby East Texas towns, working as a lease-hound for this or that oil company—mostly small independents—by the day. He chased little oil plays that flared up here and there, picking up oil leases in hot spots that glowed and often then cooled overnight with the plugging of a dry hole. But the possibilities always held excitement. Daddy hit the road with high hopes, tossing a battered leather satchel with flopping straps and a bunch of rolled-up land ownership maps into the back seat of his Ford.

In the summers, especially those summers when I was nine and ten and eleven, not old enough for real work, Daddy often took me along.

In Jacksonville, a little town thirty-five miles to the east of Athens, Daddy partnered for a while with an old man named John Lewis. For a couple of weeks we drove east from Athens in the early mornings, passing through the rolling hills and post oak flats until—just as we entered the first stands of pine trees—we hit town.

We'd always find John Lewis hunched over a cup of coffee at The Stew Pot, a cafe fronting a side street in the low-rent side of downtown. This street was a jumble, with half of the brick buildings boarded up, the rest taken up with a two-chair barber shop and a shoe repair shop and a laundry that blasted out hot puffs of steam into the heavy air.

John Lewis wore what must have been his one suit—a shabby gray one. While he talked—so low that I never could quite hear—he turned a lit cigarette with the fingers of one hand. The three of us sat at the counter, for the place was too narrow to have tables and chairs.

John Lewis was totally blind, his eyes a milky, washed-out blue that reflected nothing at all. He constantly fiddled with what was before him—his way of continually orienting himself, I figured—his hand moving from the coffee cup to the sugar container to the squat, glass vials of cream that he unerringly poured into his coffee. His universe was before him in what he could touch—he maintained those things in a certain order.

This was my first encounter with a blind person. As I spun slowly on the stool, I watched John Lewis intently. He didn't move his head when he talked or when he listened. He faced straight ahead, staring blankly toward the cream pies stacked in a glass case in front of him.

I'd close my eyes and pretend I was blind, seeing the darkness of my eyelids, and little star patterns, golden and bright when I turned towards the flyspecked plate glass window and the street.

Daddy got along great with John Lewis, admired his shrewdness, the way he could gather "dope" (this was before that word got ruined), find out where the major oil companies were taking blocks of leases. With a six-pack of bootlegged beer, he could pry the results of an overnight drillstem test out of a driller who worked the graveyard shift.

Old man Lewis' son would drop him off at the banks and the drug store coffee bar and the cafes out on the highway. He'd hang around for hours, always at the edge of the conversations, taking in the joking, the good-natured bantering and bragging, always listening. Information that he gathered could give a lease-hound a chance to bust a block by picking up a choice tract in the middle of one of the big boy's plays. Then the lease might be turned for a profit, sometimes with a minute overriding royalty interest in future production. Or the lease-hound could end up eating the lease. A high-risk business to be in.

The meetings in The Stew Pot were whispered—Daddy leaning close to John Lewis, their fedoras almost touching—and accompanied by the furtive unrolling of maps and the exchange of scribbled notes, mostly names and addresses of landowners who might be willing to sign an oil lease. Ash trays filled with cigarette butts while I whirled slowly on the red-topped stool and watched the black cook squash rounds of ground meat into hamburger patties on the grease-smeared grill.

Afterwards Daddy would chuckle lightly as we drove away. "Just a poor old blind man," he'd say. "Nobody pays him any mind. They probably feel sorry for him."

These trips for me were adventures, a glimpse of what being grown-up might someday be. Besides unlimited access to cheeseburgers and to Chocolate Soldiers—those watered-down chocolate soda pops that I loved—there was the lure of the car, the independence of the road. Maybe it was Daddy, the way he telegraphed his excitement over making a deal, his hurrying out into the country, crisscrossing the maze of deep-sand roads to buy a lease. Racing somewhere in a car foretold good news, success, the satisfaction of a job well done. Perhaps for me it defined what being a man should be. Moving around in a car became equated with moving on in life.

Even waiting in the car while Daddy ran into a bank or a title company or a county courthouse opened up opportunities to me. I felt a surge of importance, and slid across the seat to the vacant driver's side. From there I watched the action on the sidewalk, sitting tall. I rested my right wrist loosely, nonchalantly over the steering wheel, as if I had just angled the car into the parking space. I extended my left arm out the open window, tapping the top of the car coolly with my fingers, flexing my biceps, straining to hold it anytime a girl moved down the sidewalk in front of me.

On the drive back to Athens at night, with the car windows rolled down, I'd reach my arm stiffly out into the night, riding it against the air as if it were a wing and I might soar away. I'd close my eyes, savoring the coolness of the sour air when the road dipped low, rushing through the damp bottom land of the creeks. I could have ridden that way forever, or at least until breakfast.

IN THE SUMMERS of those years—if Daddy had worked most of the months before—the family would take off somewhere cool for a few days. By then there were five of us—my brother Dick, a toddler, joined Sally and me in the Ford's backseat. Most often we would head to the Texas coast, four hours south, stopping in Houston to eat at the Mexico City Cafe on South Main, a favorite place of my parents from the time we lived in that city. This was my first taste of tacos and enchiladas—pretty much ordinary Tex-Mex fare. But the place was exotic with sombreros and bullfight posters hung around and slick, red vinyl booths and mirrors all along one wall.

Daddy would dress for these rare occasions, dapper in his

one good suit and wingtip shoes. His straw dress hat sported a wide ribbon band and he cocked the hat at a jaunty angle, the style of that decade. Mother—lovely in those early days—was tall (as tall as Daddy) and slender with olive smooth skin and shoulder length black hair. She wore jewelry at special times, a string of pearls, or a brooch of amethyst. For a year or two she partnered with a sister-in-law to run the Nita-Ann Dress Shop, a narrow, deep building filled with ladies' ready-to-wear—on the square in Athens. And for those brief times style seemed to be important.

Snapshots from those years reflect an optimism that in time got squeezed out of them—when we went summer after summer without a vacation and without eating out, when all of the money—what little there was—went into cheap, East Texas scrub-oak hills and barbed wire and cedar posts for fences and corrals and bony-assed brindle cows. In those worrying-about-the-future years, faces got tight and smiles became cramped—dapper and lovely only words to capture a lost past. The jewelry stayed in the velvet-lined box on Mother's dresser.

After lunch in Houston, it was down to some isolated fishing town—often Kemah or Seabrook—where we rented a tourist cabin for the week, one room with an extra roll-away bed. It had a kitchenette so that Mother could boil shrimp and fry fish and in most all ways carry on her housewifely chores, but in a different setting.

During the early 1940s, Daddy had worked those bays and inlets, surveying lines for GSI across the shallow water for the seismic exploration that followed. He knew the territory and took great pride (landlubber that he truly was) in knowing to fish for speckled trout and redfish over reefs of shale.

We woke early the first morning there, Daddy and I off to the docks for a morning of fishing. We walked the plank pier to the end, eyeing the shrimpers cobwebbed with nets. The boats rocked quietly while gulls circled close, hoping for an early morning handout.

I enviously watched other men—other fathers and their sons—push away from the dock in sleek boats powered by massive Evinrude outboards, bamboo rods with bigger-than-your-fist reels pointing skyward optimistically. We left somewhat later, after Daddy had negotiated the best deal he could on a leaky wooden boat outfitted with a pair of oars and a salt-coated bait box. He rented two towering cane poles with tackle by the half-day and grudgingly bought a bucket of bait.

When the other boats had taken off, after the lapping of their wakes against the pier's pilings had stilled, he navigated the little wooden boat out into the bay, pulling angrily (it seemed to me) against the oars.

My job was to find the reefs of shale, probe the bottom of the bay with the butt end of a cane pole. Every few yards I pushed the pole out in front of the boat, then quickly down, hoping to feel the crunch that would alert us to a reef. "Dadgummit," Daddy said when I pulled the pole up with a glob of gray mud clinging to it. "I know there's shale out here somewhere," and he glared at me as if I were throwing him off with my awkward testing technique. He pulled hard on one of the oars, swinging us to the right or left. We'd surge forward a few yards, and he'd nod his head for me to test the bottom again.

We did find shale reefs and we did catch fish, easing our way back to the pier by noon so we could turn our tackle back in without penalty. Sunburned and sweating, we clambered out of the boat, Daddy letting me struggle with the string of a dozen or so trout, toting it the length of the pier. "Real beauties," Daddy called them. We rested at the bait shop for a while, drinking Nehi Oranges, Daddy waiting, I suspect, for some of the slick, big city fishermen in their fancy boats to motor back to the dock so he could show off what we had caught.

We cleaned the fish outside the cabin, Daddy whacking off

trout heads and slitting trout bellies in his combative slash-and-conquer way. I pulled strings of guts and sacs of eggs and other disgusting innards from the fish, then sent shiny, iridescent scales flying everywhere with the scraping of a table knife.

Mother had taken Sally and Dick to the wooden pier. It angled wobbly a hundred feet out into the shallow bay that fronted the tourist cabins. With a string and some cut bait, she filled a five-gallon bucket with enough blue-shelled crabs for dinner. In the afternoon our parents shooed us out. We three kids tumbled on the grass outside the cabin, then wandered down to the beach to chase sand crabs as they skittered to the safety of their soft-sand holes.

The rest of that trip to the coast is one of glimpses and sounds and smells: Daddy eased back into the stripes of a canvas lawn chair, sipping a beer straight from the bottle; Mother dropping crabs into the roil of an enameled pot; the pop and splatter of fish frying; the table set with a new bottle of Del Monte's Seafood Sauce—positioned to cover a cigarette burn in the oilcloth—and wedges of lemon overflowing a soft green coffee cup; plates of fried potatoes and fried trout and the tangle of the iridescent crabs.

Daddy would have another beer with supper, which created an undertone of tension in the cabin. Mother didn't confront him over this, and acted as if she hardly noticed. Maybe this was his attempt to recapture those carefree years of working with the GSI crew. But to Mother that was then, and this was now. Drinking beer was not something you did in front of your children.

Drinking openly, even a beer or two on vacation, was a step over the line, and Mother's disapproval hung thick in the steamy air, swirling and twisting with Daddy's palpable determination. We ate, the bare bulb above exposing us in harsh, yellow glare. Daddy obstinately sipped his beer.

I learned to read the levels of my life—the apparent, surface actions overlaying the roll and churn of the rapids underneath. At Mother's insistence, I recounted for the third or fourth time the probing for the reef of shale, the flash and flounce of the hooked trout in the bottom of the boat.

There was the praise for a fine meal—this from Daddy. Mother's bare nod of acceptance, her eyes averted as she single-mindedly hovered over the meal: "There's plenty of fish, I can fry some more. I should have made some hushpuppies, too. More iced tea, Sally?" And on and on, the room echoing her too-nice gestures and too-gentle voice while she busied herself with us kids and ignored Daddy. Later—her inaccessibility, her turning away, martyred to the sink full of greasy, ketchup-smeared dishes.

Daddy retreated to the porch, slapping angrily at the mosquitoes, muttering, "Dadgummit," as if the buzzing insects were the source of his torment.

That last night, the slow oscillation of the single fan swept the room, and I waited, counting the seconds it took to pass from wall to wall, back and forth, hoping that the stirring of the heavy air would bring comfort to us all.

We drove back the next day, mostly at night when it was cooler. At good dark I managed to fit myself up on the space above and behind the backseat where I lay with my nose touching the glass of the back car window. I had grown too long to fit easily there, but this is where I had ridden as a young boy, a place where the turn and grab of the rear wheels vibrated the texture of the road up through me. From there the moon passed slowly in the sky, moved from side to side as the road curved and twisted slowly to the north and I wanted the night, the sense of always moving on, to last forever.

BEING HERE ALONE, working on the seventy acres, was not a strange or alien experience, for as a boy I was always wandering and exploring.

The town of Athens, in those early years of my life, had not yet encircled our house, hemmed us in. Fields of hip-high grasses spread out behind us. Mill Run Road—a narrow, sandy lane—led south, past a hill crowded with sagging tin houses crammed with laying hens, past red clay gullies and draws that meandered back to small dug tanks loaded with red-ear perch and hand-sized bream and whiskered catfish.

I had a dog, an English setter we called Happy, who bounded before me, leading the way for my great adventures, but whose heart and nose, I now realize, belonged to the chance of encountering one of the wily coveys of quail that scurried through the fields.

I time-traveled backwards, unknowingly tapped into a hunter-gatherer atavism that subconsciously led me from fruit trees to berry thickets to lily-pad choked ponds—a compulsion that combined adventure and discovery with a basic drive for sustenance.

I gathered the first blackberries of the year that ripened along Mill Run Road about the first of June. This was a game for me—alert to every bush, every bramble, eyeing the white blossoms, the first hard green fruit, swelling and shading orange, then red, then mottled black, and finally full ripe which I dropped with red-stained fingers into a Folger's can that I would proudly present to Mother. She crushed those first-ripe berries with the back of a fork, sprinkled them generously with sugar. The next morning we spooned them over split and buttered biscuits. Praise enough, pride enough in the picking and in the eating. Worth every thorn scratch and chigger bite and seed tick.

Wild plum trees swelled with yellow and crimson fruit. I toted shiny tin syrup bucketsful to the kitchen where Mother would boil and sugar and strain until jelly the color of salmon flesh filled multifarious jars. Mother didn't use pectin and her jellies ranged from gooey to runny, but the tart sweetness is unforgettable. She canned berries and plums, peaches and pears, even citron and melon rinds and figs—all boiled and stirred while a warped-bottom pan of sterilized jars steamed up the kitchen.

With a piece of string and a fatty bacon-end, I tricked crawfish from muddy ditches, brought them home, and with no mercy stabbed an ice pick through the backs of their spiny heads and made-up waxed paper bundles of crawfish tails. Mother stuck them in the freezer, promising that when I had enough she would fry them. I don't know what ever happened to those crawfish tails.

We did eat the fish I caught, dozens and dozens, sometimes sixty or seventy bream and perch in an afternoon from a nearby pond. I cleaned them and Mother dusted them with a mixture of flour and cornmeal and fried them crispy, almost black, in a cast iron skillet.

We had a vegetable garden, Mother's project for the most part, although Daddy would fight the crab grass with his sharp hoe when things got out of hand. I weeded when I had to, but relished the harvesting, the digging of new potatoes and pulling of radishes and picking of beans.

Daddy insisted I peddle our excess vegetables in a neighborhood that had built up between our house and town. With twine I tied bundles of radishes and green onions, and filled grocery sacks with string beans and new potatoes. I dutifully pulled a wagon full of produce up and down the streets of that new subdivision, but never could work up the courage to knock on a front door.

I waited until I figured Daddy would be gone off to work and eased back to the house, sneaking the produce into the storeroom where we kept our excess potatoes spread apart to air dry on newspapers. Mother would find them there. I might get a look from her, one of disappointment, but Daddy would forget to ask how I did, I hoped. Happy and I took off for the fields.

Down Mill Run Road we went, Happy in the ditches and scrambling up the red-clay cliffs and into the woods of post oak and hickory and bright-leafed sumac and elm. With hatchet and knife I cut and shaped saplings into bows, and whittled suckers and shoots into arrows with notched shanks and finely pointed tips. I winged arrows towards cottontail rabbits and brown squirrels and even a few gravel-pecking doves, and discovered that I was more gatherer than hunter.

At the dusty edges of the road I did find other things—illicit discoveries that quickened something deep inside of me, something I couldn't label at that time. Bottles and cans littered the roadside; the fresh ones, tossed there from last Saturday night, still held a residue of red wine or clear gin or amber whiskey. There were crumpled cans of Jax and Pabst and Falstaff.

I smelled them all, sniffed the liquid mystery that was forbidden in this county, and in the counties adjoining. From Athens it was sixty miles to the rough and tumble oil towns of Kilgore or Gladewater—and their liquor stores. It was even a few miles farther to the outskirts of Dallas. Anything that difficult to get must be special, I figured.

In a shaded pull-off down the road, I poked at a shriveled rubber with a stick, shivering with anticipation or dread, as if I were easing to the edge of a red-clay bluff blindfolded, wanting to find the edge with my toes, to experience the vertigo, but not fall. Not yet.

Back home I climbed the oak tree behind our house, from where I could survey the fields to the south. Back to the east I watched our neighbor's house, hoping that Judy Barlow might be around and would come over and play. Judy was eight, a year younger than I, and willing to help build tee-pees out of slender sassafras poles tied with twine at the top, layered with bunches of red-stemmed grass. Sometimes we just played chase, but once we developed our side yard into a miniature golf course.

An uncle had left a wooden-handled putter and a couple of grass-stained golf balls at our house, which presented this young entrepreneur with an opportunity not to be overlooked. In the yard next to Mill Run Road, in and around the trees, I dug holes with a butcher knife and scraped the "fairways" clean, while Judy printed the sign—"MINIATURE GOLF 10 CENTS"—with three colors of Crayolas. We hung around our golf course for a couple of days, alert to every car that drove by, but the second night Happy dug a sleeping place in the fresh scraped dirt around the third hole and we took the sign down.

Judy's father, Lawrence Barlow, was a gentle sort of man, tall, with prematurely thinning hair, a little out of place in Athens, it now seems to me. He raised pigeons in a coop in his backyard, and late summer evenings quartets of gray and white pigeons circled over our roof coming back to roost in the pen behind his house.

Lawrence managed the A&P that took up one corner of the downtown square. Helen, his wife, worked checkout at the store. She was tall and attractive in a dark-eyed, middle-European gypsy sort of way. Mother always liked Lawrence better than Helen, probably not ever at ease with Helen's dubious, non-Confederate origins.

The Barlows got a television set a couple of years before we did. One night a week they asked me over to watch the wrestling matches. We gathered around the black and white screen and booed Duke Keomuka with his judo chops, and Danny Savage with his illegal stranglehold. We cheered as Lou Thesz time and again defended his World Championship title. After the matches he strode around the ring, arms defiantly shaking at the heavens, sporting the biggest, gaudiest championship belt imaginable.

Judy and I grew out of that childhood friendship. Adolescence made being pals more complicated. After high school I pretty much lost contact with her.

In the sixties, a modern A&P opened up out on the highway south of Athens to meet the new competition of Piggly Wiggly and Brookshire Brothers. Lawrence raised appaloosa horses by then, his new salary elevating him above the pigeon-breeding bracket, I guess. Sometimes when I returned to Athens for Thanksgiving or Christmas or for an uncle's funeral, I would make a point to stop by the supermarket and say hi to the Barlows. But things were not as they appeared.

Late one night a distraught Lawrence Barlow found Helen snuggled up next to Bill Henderson in his telephone company pickup parked under the canopy of a local root beer stand. Lawrence made some sort of threat—something I can't quite imagine—and Bill Henderson drew a pistol from under the truck seat and shot him in the stomach. Lawrence Barlow bled to death on the spot.

I never heard the Barlows mentioned again in our house. It was to Mother as if they never existed, had not been her closest neighbors for twenty years. I asked once—about Judy, about Helen—but all I got was a tight-lipped turnaway and silence.

ONE MORNING I PICKED UP something in the air, some conflict between Mother and Daddy that I'm sure wasn't new to them, but that day for me things shifted. Daddy paced around the house, from the kitchen where Mother busied herself at the sink to the back porch and down to their bedroom. He walked hard, fast, only to stride back through the bright kitchen once more, and down the length of the living room and then back again.

I was in the backyard, checking on Happy, who was listless, had for some reason stopped leading me on my daily explorations, and now stood spraddle-legged in the shade wheezing. I tried to comfort Happy, running my hand over the black and white spots on his back, but when I tried to force him to lie down, he whimpered and I stopped.

The argument from the house, as I heard it develop, had to do with money, but it went deeper than money this time, for there never was, never had been quite enough money, or certainly not its surety. But this time the words from Mother cut deeper, sliced into areas of regret, of hopes and expectations and disappointments. Houston was mentioned, a place Mother always loved, with its promise to elevate her above the country-poor way she was brought up.

Earlier in the afternoon, Mother's other sister Inez, and her husband Walt had stopped by our house for coffee. Inez and Walt now lived only a few blocks away in that new development where I took my vegetables for a wagon ride. But Walt had made some money in West Texas drilling water wells out around Midland, and you got the feeling that they considered being around Athens slightly beneath them. But every few years, for whatever reason, they left the oil boom and bust of the Permian Basin and settled around Athens, closer to their kin for short stretches of time.

Inez dropped by the house dressed—if you could call it that, more costumed—in a dressing gown of sorts, some flimsy, layered outfit of chiffon and satin, covering her shoulders with a padded satin wrap that tied with silk bows in the front. Her shiny black hair fell in a wave, a la Lana Turner, almost to one eye. Inez reclined on Mother's chartreuse sofa, stuck a Pall Mall in a gold-plated cigarette holder, and lit up with a loopy smile. I suspect she lunched on sherry or popped some sedative for her nerves. Relaxation never seemed to be an issue with Inez.

The three Baxter sisters covered the territory of character types. Mother's other, and oldest sister, Aunt Dee Dee (born Fannie Louise, a name she abhorred—the Fannie part, especially—called Madam Queen by her husband, Uncle Frank, a name I hope she never heard) was pale of skin, thin of lip, quick with tongue, and—armed with her twin Bibles—rigid with beliefs. The Devil himself ventured across Aunt Dee Dee's boundaries at his own peril.

Inez, the middle sister, had the same olive complexion as Mother, the same dark hair and strong bones—an attractive woman to anyone's eye. Uncle Walt called her "Lady," which pretty well paints the picture. Afford it or not, Lady shopped Neiman Marcus in Dallas, sipped a little French wine in the evenings, ate Chateaubriand and spoke of cherries jubilee. She and Walt collected antiques—European antiques. For Lady, life lay ripe with pleasures to be plucked, the promise of luxury, and fine gifts to be savored.

Mother had resigned herself—for the most part, for most of the times—to much less. She did still have dreams, Houston sorts of dreams, for she painted the pine floors in their bedroom black and bought, at a closeout sale, crushed red velvet-covered chairs and matching, armless chartreuse sofas for the living room. I'm sure she would have loved an Oriental rug to cover the rough pine living room floor.

And Daddy always had one good suit, bought at Titches or Sanger Harris in downtown Dallas, and one good pair of wingtip shoes, and a snappy fedora. From the mid-1950s on, we had a Buick for the main family car. Daddy was torn, I'm sure, between sprigging a deep-sand pasture with coastal Bermuda grass and putting up the cash for a new car. But, in the end, his sincere belief that appearing successful would lead to success won out.

But their day in and day out reality ground Mother down. Days of Penney's sale dresses, and sewing my school shirts and Sally's blouses. No chateaubriand, but Swiss steak butchered from one of Daddy's grass-fed steers, round steak braised until it finally broke down and fell apart in the skillet.

Mother had moved on past milking a Jersey cow we staked in the backyard that first year or so in Athens. But still Doom and Destruction and Poverty awaited. Life for Mother forever remained the "long road with no turning."

An hour or two of her sister—with Walt lighting Lady's cigarettes and freshening her coffee, and Lady planning another trip to Neimans—left Mother justly frazzled and frustrated. But Inez was her older sister, and with Inez directing the action from the sofa, Mother reverted to being the little sister.

For me, Walt and Inez enlarged the possibilities. They possessed a calm dignity and self assurance. Walt could drill wells and repair antiques and slide in and out of the world of oil money with ease. He was articulate, his voice full and rich and always gentle. Their daughter Enid would in a few years marry (and not too many years later divorce) an honest-to-God movie star, who I later glimpsed on the big screen in brief supporting roles in second-rate Westerns.

I couldn't imagine Walt and Inez ever, ever arguing about stretching dollars here or there. Inez sewing her daughter's clothes? Canning jelly? Straining to open barbed wire gates for Walt to drive his shiny car through? Walt charging groceries at the Red Top store, or hauling a bale of hay around in the trunk of his car? Unthinkable.

After Walt and Inez left, Daddy found himself in a bind, and he defended himself as best he could. "Now, Talkie, you know this," he said, and "Now, dadgummit, Talkie, you know that." The fine points of the disagreement evaded me, but it boiled down to

Mother being tired of living week to week, and tired of Daddy not having steady work in the cyclical rise and fall of the oil business. And in those lean times, frustrated by his inactivity, Daddy kept diverting scarcer and scarcer funds to barbed wire and then a pricey bull, and otherwise dribbling what little money we had into the sink hole of his cow/calf operation.

In the face of this conflict, my flight syndrome clicked in, but Happy was there, panting hard, and somehow I couldn't leave him alone. But when the argument got more intense I slipped back to my room, where Dick was busy throwing stuffed animals and wooden trucks one at a time from his crib to the floor. I would have closed the door to our room if there had been one. Sally was in her room, at the other end of the hall. She had a door and it was closed, but I could hear her radio. I tried to concentrate on a balsa wood B-17 model that seemed to have a missing wing flap, but I couldn't shut the voices out.

"I can't even go to the grocery store," Mother said, her voice strong, carrying easily from the kitchen. Mother did not whine.

"Go to the Red Top," Daddy said, knowing that Dee Tyner would let Mother charge her groceries there. He kept a stack of charge booklets rubber-banded together in a drawer.

"Dee Tyner's a thief," Mother said. "And I will not trade there. You can, if you want to. If you have to have your cigarettes."

"Dadgummit, Talkie," Daddy said, and I could feel, all the way back in my room, Mother shushing him, afraid I would hear them fight, and Daddy's voice got lower.

I went to my bank, a yellow and orange and brown costumed tin monkey that tipped his hat every time you dropped a coin in, and emptied it on the bed. Thirty-six cents.

Mother and Daddy got quiet when I came back to the kitchen. Mother wouldn't face me, and I knew she had been crying. Daddy looked desperate, and I could tell he wanted me out of there.

I handed him my money. "I know it's not much," I said, "but it's all I have, and it will buy some bread or milk or something, and Happy is sick, something's bad wrong with him." I began to cry, and then I left, ran out into the field to the grass covered tee-pee Judy Barlow and I had built, and with my knife I stabbed out a hole in the soft ground. I sat there for a long time, imagining that the tee-pee was somewhere out West, in the mountains, and that I lived there alone, or with only Happy, and we hunted and fished and never needed any money.

In a little while, the car door slammed and Daddy backed his Ford out of the driveway, then headed up the Cayuga highway. To the Red Top for cigarettes, I figured. But it was for more—at supper we splurged on a sirloin steak that hung over the edges of the platter, cooked gray all the way through, and baked potatoes slippery with Oleo. Chocolate Mellorine for dessert.

I salvaged the steak bone and a little fat for Happy. He sniffed at it, licked the fat with his tired tongue, but wouldn't eat. Happy still wouldn't lie down, so in the storeroom I found a cardboard box that I cut down and slid underneath his belly for support. Mother gave me back my thirty-six cents, explaining that sometimes grown-ups worry more than they should. Daddy wasn't around.

I sat on the grass next to Happy until dark when Mother came out and knelt beside us both. She patted Happy gently and shook her head. She told me it was bedtime.

In the morning, Happy lay stiffly on his side, next to the tipped-over box. A little crust of blood stuck at the corner of his mouth, and a few flies buzzed around his shallow, open eyes. Daddy wrapped Happy in a burlap tow sack and buried him in the back corner of the garden. I wandered out to the tee-pee, lost. I could still go out West to the mountains, but now I would have to go alone.

Saturday: Day Six

I WOKE UP LATE, possessed by a just-before-waking dream that wouldn't leave me alone. In this dream my Uncle Slats and Aunt Maxine were fighting, yelling at each other. Finally Slats started cramming hot dogs, buns and all (not just cold wieners, which made more sense) into Maxine's mouth, but still she yelled at him, with mustard dripping from the corners of her mouth.

I splashed my face with water and crawled through the barbed wire fence and onto the dirt road that ran along the south side of the pasture, sprinting a few hundred yards until I was winded. Then I jogged back to my camp through the stasis of gray dust I had raised.

The unpleasantness of the dream led me to another image, this one of Slats at rest in his open casket. My mother had driven me to the funeral home the night before the burial. We moved into a shadowed parlor with sprays of gladioluses and mums all around. A couple of my older cousins from Kerens were there, the men in the family having made out a schedule so that at least one of them would be at the funeral home throughout the night to "sit up" with the body.

These two cousins were uncharacteristically dressed up in navy blue slacks and white dress shirts with the sleeves turned twice and clip-on ties. I hardly recognized them. They had been sitting, leaning forward, heads close together and arguing about something, but got quiet and nodded and sat up straight when Mother and I walked in.

My mother leaned sadly over the casket and gave her dead brother a little kiss on the cheek. She didn't cry then, but firmly took my hand and pulled me close to the casket to see. Slats looked good, a little paler than most times, but more at ease than I had ever seen him. Death, I guess, does that to you, but I was only twelve and death still surprised me. My mother looked at Slats and then at me. She nodded her head as if she were saying, "See this, Donnie, this is what it all comes down to." She always said that "life is a long road with no turning." I accepted this as a truism, which it is, but later it was her warning, intended to scare me back into the Church of Christ fold. And it did scare me a little, yes, but not back into any church.

My problems with the church were less complex, more pragmatic. I went to the chief elder a couple of times with problems—big problems. A church baseball league was starting up and I wanted to play. But Mother stiffened when I asked to try out for the Baptist Braves or the Presbyterian Panthers. So I counted up the boys in church and figured we could scrape together a team, and ran that idea by Chief Elder. He, literally, patted me on the head, gave me his pious, condescending smile, and quoted some verse about avoiding "the things of the world."

I knew better. There was no prohibition against baseball anywhere in the Bible—and with that my disenchantment began to creep in. Eternity in hell seemed improbable, but death still bothered me.

My mother's own mother would die within the next year, at our house, in an added-on room next to the carport. Mommy, as we kids called her, lay sick in our house for more than two years, bedridden most of the time. Mother nursed her, cooked vegetables and roast beef until they fell apart so Mommy could chew them. Once a day Mother went out into our backyard and cut a slender elm branch ("piss elum," my daddy said) and stripped its bark. Mommy used that to clean her teeth. I guess it worked, for she died with her full mouth of teeth intact.

Now I forced myself back to work, aware that this was Saturday and I only had the rest of today before Daddy would pass judgment on the stacks of mesquite. But death still haunted me, and under every tree I imagined a rabbit, blending into the grass, waiting for me to butcher it.

After lunch I sharpened my axe and leaned back against a bois d'arc tree for a little rest that I had trouble rising from. I fought off sleep, afraid of the dreams that might revisit me, afraid that the piles of mesquite would not measure up to Daddy's expectations. But sleep won out.

The sound of a truck startled me awake sometime later. I scrambled to my feet, and got busy filling the sprayer with diesel fuel, trying to act nonchalant. The last thing I needed was for somebody to report back to Daddy that I was asleep on the job. I didn't look up even when the truck stopped at the barbed wire gap and a door slammed, but then I heard a racking cough and knew it was my Uncle Frank.

Shit, I thought—a few months back I had come home after school to what I thought was an empty house and found Frank passed out on our back porch. As a young man Frank had been imposing—his nickname was "Heavy"—but now, in his mid-fifties, he had been shrunken by emphysema, although he still carried a rough and tough reputation. Frank worked as a roughneck and then a driller on oil rigs until a Stilson wrench that dropped from the top of a derrick dented his hard hat and jammed the vertebrae in his neck.

The afternoon I had found him on our back porch, he was out cold, but as I knelt over him his eyelids fluttered open. All he said before passing back into unconsciousness was, "I'm gonna kill you." It scared the pee out of me. With shaking hands I dialed the local hospital and they sent an ambulance out. The driver got Frank awake and gave a little laugh. "Hell, he's drunk, boy," was all he said before he left.

It turned out that Frank wasn't drunk at all, but had suffered a mild stroke or heart attack. But what stuck with me from that day on was, "I'm gonna kill you."

Frank didn't have much to do now. He drew a little disability, a little social security, I guess. He lived with my Aunt Dee Dee in a frame house near the high school. This is the house he bought for them when Dee Dee had her appendix out. While she recuperated in the hospital, Uncle Frank sold their nice, big house over on East Tyler Street. She never forgave Uncle Frank for this, but that transgression was just one in what must have been a long line of unforgivable transgressions.

I had early on heard the story of how Uncle Frank, as a younger man, got a good job in a Wyoming oil field and Dee Dee took the train up there to join him. She stayed one day (and night, I guess) with him before catching the next train right back to Texas.

Frank and Dee Dee never had children and I suspect the problem wasn't infertility so much as infrequency. Like maybe never. Or maybe once or twice, so that Dee Dee could confirm what she suspected about that distasteful, messy act. Dee Dee's body language told it all. She sat in her living room, rocking in her high-back chair with her legs crossed, her arms crossed, and her hair bobby-pinned up in tight ringlets so she would look good at church on Sunday.

Dee Dee had two Holy Bibles—one on a table to her left, the other on a table to her right—as if she were a gunfighter and the Bibles her six-shooters. They were always within easy reach, a forbidding challenge for any man, even a character as rough as Uncle Frank.

Frank was slow to pull his pickup through the wire gap and then close it behind him. Finally he eased the pickup towards me, the truck rocking from side to side as it rode the imprints of forgotten cotton rows across the pasture. He stopped on the east side of the bois d'arc grove in a particularly dense patch of shade. He swung the truck door open and—stiffnecked—nodded my way. He pushed his hat back on his head and methodically rolled a Bull Durham cigarette. All the time he had a little smile on his face, a smile that was not a real smile, more of a grin that he wouldn't allow to reach the surface.

I poured a half-jar of water and reluctantly made my way to his truck, a green Chevy he had driven as long as I could remember. When I got near the tailgate, I stopped and leaned warily against the side of the truck. I knew I could outrun Frank and would be out of danger as long as I stayed these few safe steps away. Unless he had a gun—which rumor had it he carried in his truck.

Frank nodded again, held out his pouch of tobacco, his packet of rolling papers. I shook my head, bent down and picked some needle grass out of my socks, furtively watching Frank out of the corner of my eye.

"Have a smoke," he said. "I won't tell D.E." He reached the tobacco towards me again. "Hell, I'll roll one for you."

I liked it when Frank called Daddy "D.E." Somehow it turned Daddy into a person, as if he were just another of Frank's cronies and not someone whose approval I needed.

"I would, you know," I said. "Cigarettes are okay, but I need to stay in shape for football."

Frank shook his head, best he could, in obvious disgust. He looked past me then, out across the field of my week's work, that grin coming back onto his leathery face. "Clearing a little mesquite, huh?" he said. "Looks like about two days of cutting to me. What did you do the other two days? Stump break one of them heifers? Lope your mule?" He gave a shallow laugh, followed by a deep storm of coughs, a glob of yellow mucus spat to one side. Frank wiped his arm across his mouth and sat there panting like an overheated dog.

I turned away, studied the piles of brush. Frank laughed again, a laugh that started up another one of his coughing fits. I thought he might fall out of the pickup coughing and gasping for breath, and I swore that if he did I wouldn't go near him, wouldn't touch him or help him at all. I'd let him die right there in that needle grass pasture and not mind one bit.

Finally Frank turned and found a bottle of something amber on the seat beside him and took a couple of quick swallows between his coughing spasms. In a minute he got quiet, breathing heavily. I could see the sweat on his forehead. He had a faraway look in his eyes, as if he had been somewhere, seen something that disturbed him.

When he spoke again, his words fell between his shallow breaths. "Come on," he said, "go with me over to Prairie Point." He tilted his head east, back up the road behind him.

I shook my head, mumbled something about the work I was doing, that Daddy might be over after a while. The truth was that Frank scared me and there was no way I would crawl in that pickup with him, even to go the six or seven miles over to the Prairie Point cemetery. I had been to Prairie Point a dozen times or more, for that was where all of my ancestors, back four or five generations on both sides, were buried.

When I hesitated, Frank grumbled, "We won't be long. I need

you to help me with something. I'll take care of D.E. Don't worry." Now he had lost that half-hidden grin, and I knew he meant it. He did need my help. "You can drive," he said then, and I knew I was a goner. He swung his legs back in the pickup and slid across the seat, leaving the driver's side for me.

Life is filled with temptations, more on down the road than I could have ever imagined. But at fourteen a chance to drive a 1949 Chevy pickup the seven miles and back on those black-dirt country roads ranked right up there with the most attractive of them.

I turned up the jar of water I carried, gulped it dry, and rolled it like a bowling ball back across the needle grass toward my campsite. From behind the steering wheel, I glanced around a minute, surreptitiously, but couldn't spot a gun.

I nonchalantly started the truck, revved it a few times, and managed to back it away from the trees with a minimum of jerking. Once out on the road and in third gear I felt confident enough to drive with one hand, my left arm resting lightly out the open window.

On the way over, Frank caught me up on an invention he about had perfected—a perpetual motion machine that he kept locked up in a shed out behind his house. He got that sly grin back on his face, twiddled with a Bull Durham pouch while he talked. "Yes, siree," he said, "the big boys, Humble and Magnolia and Sinclair, they'll throw a shit-fit when this thing hits the market. Good-bye, internal combustion engine." He hesitated a moment. "Now don't go and tell this to D.E." I swore I wouldn't.

On a curve of the road towards the cemetery we suddenly came upon a stark church building. I slowed, looking off to my right, past Frank, while still managing to stay more or less in the soft give of the ruts. The church yard was the color of fireplace ash, but hard-scraped and clean-swept to keep a dry-grass summer fire from engulfing it. Plainness was a virtue around there. Or simply a necessity.

One summer, several years before, when Sally and I had spent a few weeks with Aunt Dee Dee, the three of us had walked the mile from Dee Dee's house, wandering down that dusty road to this very church each Sunday. Uncle Frank was off somewhere, escaped to freedom and the good pay of an oil field job, and, besides, he wouldn't have been caught alive inside a church at that time.

The white-painted siding and clear glass windows of the building shimmered beneath the wood shingle roof. Inside, the floor stretched longways with broad-planked pine. A dozen straight-backed pews were lined up on either side of the middle aisle that ended at a potbellied wood stove. In the summer it still held an odor of sour ash.

There were a few worn hymnals to share, stuck in the slatted pew-back racks or carelessly scattered on the seats. A funeral home in Kerens had donated hand-held fans with a mournful, long-haired Jesus and a couple of lambs on one side, and the mortuary name and phone number on the other. The fans were made of thin paper glued to a skinny wooden frame, the handle much like an oversized popsicle stick.

Fan technique fascinated me. There were the rapid-fanners, mostly heavy-set, stiff-backed, pious-looking women who rested the fan across their laps, then, in a manic flurry, waved the fan in front of their faces for a minute or so, and then, just as suddenly, stopped.

The true country women, those who had milked their Jersey cows at daybreak, and baked biscuits in the wood stove, and left yeast rolls rising while they worshipped the Lord—these women slumped in the pews, grateful for the time of rest from the rigors of their lives and fanned themselves unceasingly throughout the service—languidly, steadily—moving the fan just enough to keep a little air stirring.

I tried to figure out which method was most effective. The rapid swishing stirred more air, without doubt, but the effort had to raise the body temperature, counteracting the cooling action. The slow fanning barely gave comfort, but required little energy. Later, I asked Dee-Dee what she thought, but she dismissed me with a "hmphh." She didn't approve of either technique, it seemed, or either group of women. Or maybe she didn't know the answer.

Answers bothered me, but for the most part I went along with things without question. In the Church of Christ, baptism isn't for infants, not something imposed upon squalling babies, but a deliberate act reserved for that time when you reach the "age of accountability." That age of knowing right from wrong and having enough "what for" to make a rational decision was judged to occur at about twelve years of age. This was the custom of those church folks, and one that made sense within their paradigms.

But I slid through my twelfth year without making a move, not being tempted whatsoever by the desperately pleading songs that ended (before the final prayer) all three services of the week. And the threats of eternal hell fire and banishment to live with the very real devil didn't move me.

Mother never said a word, although I could feel her nudging me, bring up how wonderful it was to see those kids my age move out into the aisle and allow themselves to be dunked in the baptistery behind the pulpit.

Somehow she blamed my recalcitrance on the preacher we had at the time, a Brother Bob Love, who preached everything but love.

As the months passed, Mother got steamed up more and more at Brother Love, blaming him for this and for that, small stuff that even I figured were just stand-ins for his inability to move me to be saved.

Finally she saw her opportunity and faced it head on. Brother Love was out of town, taking a week's vacation ("Don't know why a preacher needs a vacation," Daddy humphed. "They don't ever put in a day's work.") And Kermit Upshaw—one in a succession of preachers from the church's past—would stand in on Sunday. And Mother, desperate, I guess, for the fate of my soul, for once attacked the problem directly. She took me aside before church, told me that she understood why I had put off being baptized, that she wouldn't care to be dunked by that Brother Love either. But Brother Upshaw, he was different, and she knew that I would understand the seriousness of my condition.

Mostly to get out from under Mother's disappointment, I dragged myself up front during the last verse of the last hymn, right after the "Why do you wait, dear brother?" part. The good sisters of the congregation cried while Brother Upshaw led me to a back room. There I stripped all the way and got into a too-short white robe, more a hemmed sheet than anything else. I got dunked in the presence of that ragtag bunch of Church of Christers, before Whomever it might concern. My biggest worry, coming back up out of those cleansing waters, was that my privates would show through the wet gown.

Around the next curve—Frank silent, smoking beside me—we came upon my Uncle Gee and Aunt Ola's place, just across the road from where Aunt Dee Dee and Uncle Frank used to live. Frank never looked up at the old Baxter homeplace, as if he had never lived there, but instead nodded towards Uncle Gee's, motioning for me to stop there.

Uncle Gee had a dog named Buck, who—at his command—would attack a rope that dangled from a front yard pear tree. Buck growled and snarled and swung from that rope until the day's ripe pears thudded to the scraped-bare yard. Uncle Gee rewarded Buck with a chunk of "dog bread," some wood-stove, hard-baked cornmeal concoction that Uncle Gee could never convince me to try.

We got a cool drink from their well, Uncle Gee dropping the shiny tin pail into the darkness of the hand-dug well, down past the jug of milk he stored there, until it splashed. He waited a minute for the bucket to tilt and sink and fill. He spit some tobacco to one side while he held his hand on the crank, and then wound up the bucket, splashing full.

We took turns sipping from a shiny metal dipper that hung on a nail above the well. There was a protocol, an etiquette to this. You never drank the last of the water from the dipper, but left enough in the bottom to swirl and splash out onto the dirt, so you could hand it clean to the next person. I never figured out if the water tasted metallic, or if it was the dipper, the metal on my lips. But the water was cold and hard enough almost to bite.

My Great-Uncle Gee was a quiet man. He and Frank mostly grunted by way of conversation. As we left I waved to Aunt Ola who had stepped out onto the front porch, drying her hands on her apron.

Prairie Point cemetery lies at the end of that dirt road—the last stop, you might say. It is a soft and lovely place, an oasis of sorts in the bleakness of that mostly barren cotton land. Oak trees have shaded the grounds for more than a century, and makeshift tables have been fabricated out of rough-cut two-by-twelves secured from tree to tree in a grove next to the burial grounds. There must be three or four hundred graves, the gravestones relating their stories, connected in obtuse and overlapping ways. On the hottest July day of the year more than two dozen extended families whose ancestors are laid to rest at Prairie Point gather for a combination picnic, family reunion, and cemetery fundraiser.

I slowed the pickup to a crawl, guided it to a patch of shade, and almost killed it before I remembered to hit the clutch. We sat there a moment, Frank now quiet, taking it all in. Then with a cough he motioned me on through a gate. I guided the truck slowly around to the back of the cemetery where he told me to stop.

"I'm thinking about right over there," he said, pointing towards a pomegranate tree already thick with just-turning fruit. There were no other graves around that area.

I could see Frank's dilemma. For this was not his place, but a place of Watts and Baxters, Kirks and Bounds. He would be a stranger here among the dead. But he had no other place.

"Now, you remember this. You understand? Do I need to mark the spot?"

I gazed out the window, past Uncle Frank, over the tops of all of those modest grave markers of limestone and gray granite and wood. "I'll remember," I said. "Next to the pomegranate tree. But why don't you just tell Dee Dee? Wouldn't that be better?"

Frank cut his eyes back at me. "Madam Queen?" He dragged a kitchen match under the dash of the truck. It popped with a yellow flame. He lit his wrinkled cigarette and took a shallow drag. "Shit," he grunted, "she don't give a flying fart." Then he grinned. "You'll see. About women. One of these days."

We sat there quiet after that, Frank slowly smoking, letting the ashes fall between his legs to the floorboard of the truck, his breath shallow wheezes.

I looked around. All of those mounds marking graves. There were all sizes—little baby graves and long slender graves, there were single brick headstones and marble and granite headstones. Some of the graves were marked with only a rusted-wire flower container. To walk the cemetery was to know the epidemics of the past century, the flu viruses that swept across the country in waves every other generation, the wars from the 1860s on.

I tried to spot where my mother's daddy was buried, the graves of his parents nearby, a vacant spot next to it waiting for my grandmother.

And on my daddy's side, there were graves that went back four generations. One I remembered—a James Watt, born in Devonshire, England in 1824. To end up here, with bare ground all around for more. Another Watt, my grandfather, would be laid there within three years. Yes, with bare ground all around for more. I tried to visualize the length of eternity, but it eluded me. My head spun. I grasped the steering wheel tighter, determined to hang on, as long as I could.

My mother was right. Life is a long road with no turning. She dared to peer down that road and spotted the end. Frank saw it, too. And it wasn't so far away.

On the way back Frank sat quietly, gazing out his open window. The ash from his cigarette grew long and finally fell to the floorboard. The road back to the seventy acres seemed long, the joy of driving his pickup sucked out of me, out through the open window into the superheated air.

I was glad to be alone again, back among the mesquite with my axe, working, trying to slash my way through the thicket that surrounded me.

After every few swings of the axe I stopped, listening for the sound of Daddy's car, afraid he might come over early to check on me. On the one hand, I desperately wanted to make up for the time I had lost this afternoon. I attacked the trees with feverish energy. And I got smart, started picking and choosing the mesquites with the fewest sprouts, or trees that when hacked down would leave a sizable clearing around them to give the illusion of covering more territory.

But on the other hand, I was almost past caring, for I was down to the dregs of my water, the bottom quarter of the ten gallon can. And somehow—at times I had stood there drinking with the lid off, I figured—some unidentifiable bugs and tiny seeds found their way into the insulated can and now clung onto a filmy layer of transparent scum that coated the water.

I dreamed of iced tea, tall icy glasses with lots of sugar to stir up from the bottom. Endless glasses of iced tea. And I dreamed of food, Mother's food. I couldn't wait for Sunday, for even on ordinary Sundays—after a breakfast of buttermilk biscuits (not light and fluffy, but chewy and a little sour) and sausage patties and wild plum jelly and velvety ribbon cane syrup—Mother mixed up a batch of yeast rolls and left them to rise, covered with a dish towel on top of the stove. She cut up a fryer and crisped it dark brown in an inch of shortening that splattered and sizzled in an oversize cast-iron skillet. She stuck the chicken platter in the oven where the pilot light would keep it warm while we drove into town to Sunday school and church.

She peeled Irish potatoes and left them covered in a pot of cold water so they wouldn't turn, and so they would be ready with the twist of a burner knob and the flick of a match to boil and mash and cream and butter and salt and pepper when we returned. On Saturday she would have baked a cobbler from fresh berries or peaches or apples, Crisco-flaky around the edges, and rich, the fruit juices oozing through and staining the low spots of the crust.

Mother set the table with her Desert Rose china and pattern-worn-smooth silver-plated tableware. If we had company, one of Mother's brothers and his family, or maybe Uncle Walt and Lady, or Aunt Dee Dee if Uncle Frank was off somewhere, then we struggled with the table, pulling it apart, adding a leaf or two to accommodate the visitors.

If it was just us then Daddy got me or Sally to say the blessing, the standard, "God is great, God is good, let us thank Him for this food. Amen." If we had company, Daddy would say the prayer, his mumble only a degree or two more comprehensible than his own father's had been, and just as brief.

Summer Sundays were the best, for there would be a platter

of sliced tomatoes and a bowl of peas—blackeyes or purple hulls or cream peas—cooked with the green snaps too skinny to shell, and a chunk of brown-rind slab bacon. Maybe a platter of home-canned pickles and pickled peaches, the bowl of hot rolls covered with a cloth, and a plate of corn bread sticks for good measure. The mashed potatoes stood stiff and high in the bowl with a big square of butter melting on top. There was salt and pepper in shakers, and a bottle of homemade pepper sauce to sprinkle over the peas. A Desert Rose sugar bowl mounded up to sweeten the tall glasses of strong iced tea.

Mother and Daddy would have coffee with the cobbler. Daddy loaded both the tea and coffee with sugar, two or three heaping teaspoons. Mother always frowned when he did that, but hardly ever said anything. If she did, it would be to blame Granny for having always oversweetened everything.

I dreamed of other meals my mother made. We ate from the garden, green beans, boiled with a piece of pork fat until they were limp, and skin-on new potatoes, and fall-apart pot roast or a bone-in ham.

Lunches were simpler, baloney and sliced tomatoes and Miracle Whip on white-bread sandwiches with icicle radishes and slender green onions from the garden, and maybe a pot of pinto beans cooked with a scrap piece of ham until they were soupy and thick. For dessert, Del Monte fruit cocktail, or canned pear halves with a chunk of cream cheese in the center.

And suppers of spaghetti smothered with a meat and tomato sauce, topped with rough slices of melted rat-trap cheese; or Swiss steak that no amount of cooking could ever tenderize, the beef brought home in frozen, white, paper-wrapped blocks from City Market in town where we rented a locker to hold the grass-fattened calf that Daddy had processed once a year.

There was always dessert—in the evenings a cream pie or a

layer cake or a frozen cream cheese and mayonnaise and canned fruit cocktail concoction that stuck to the roof of your mouth. Sometimes an imitation ice cream mix that Mother stirred up and froze in an ice cube tray, a special treat that turned to dirty foam in your bowl when it melted.

Food dreams kept me going that last day, for I was sick of peanut butter, sick of lukewarm cans of pork and beans and slippery sardines. I had failed to tighten the top on the pint of plum jelly, and ants had discovered that sweet stickiness. Not just a few ants, either, which I would have picked out and flicked away, but hundreds upon hundreds of tiny black ants that clamored feverishly in huge, black moving clumps, covering the jar completely. In disgust I kicked the jar as hard as I could towards the fence line. Ants went everywhere.

That evening, just at dusk, I took a stick of Vienna sausage saved from my supper and a piece of string and tried my luck at crawfishing in the muddy tank. On the way there I met the herd of cows on the narrow path they had worn deep in the weeds. I moved to one side and let them pass. Mud coated their still-wet legs, and flies made black carpets across their backs—carpets that lifted and moved and reconfigured with the rhythmic swishing of their tails.

Crawfish lived in the mud of the tank, for towers made of mud clumps were scattered here and there along the murky water's edge. I tied the Vienna sausage on one end of a string and tossed it out. I eased down on the hard-clod ground and waited for some action, waited for a crawfish to start nibbling at the bait so I could gently lift it from the water and onto the shore.

In the distance a tractor moved silently across the horizon, plowing under a field of stunted corn stalks, maybe, or topping the weeds in a dried-out pasture. The sun set behind the tractor as I watched. In a few minutes deep purple shadows crept towards me across the field, finally shrouding the tank where I sat, then taking in the whole seventy acres.

A little breeze picked up right at dark and while I watched, the tractor lights flashed on. I wondered what the man on the tractor was thinking. Maybe he had seen me earlier, when the sun would have glistened against the white of my T-shirt. I might have been a speck that caught his eye and he would have been curious about that lone figure lost in the field of mesquite.

Or maybe he was worrying about money, how he would pay for new seed to plant or gas for his tractor, and maybe he worked late because he dreaded going to his house where his wife would question him. "What are we going to do?" she might ask, all worried and crying and angry, and he would have no answers.

Or maybe she waited for him, a big jolly woman with a pan of meatloaf still warm in the oven and cornbread sticks with lots of butter and a tall glass of sweet iced tea and a berry cobbler for dessert. And they would talk about the fine things of their lives, the joy he got from driving his own tractor, and the woman, proud of jars of summer tomatoes she had put up that day, and, later, they would go to bed and hold each other, or whatever—things became murky right there—and be happy if only the breeze kept up and cooled the house and let them sleep.

I looked back down at my feet to check the string with the Vienna sausage bait, but it was gone. Finally, I spotted it, the last few inches of white string floating on the dark water, slowly moving away from me, dragged off by a hungry crawfish, I figured.

The moon had started to rise in the east and I easily picked up the cow trail that led back to the bois d'arc thicket. I kept my eye on the trail, stepping around fresh cow plops, but still managed to watch the steady movement of tractor lights, back and forth in the distance, until I entered the solitude of the bois d'arc woods. It's not easy out here, not for a man on a tractor or for a crawfish. Not for a boy cutting mesquite, either.

Burning: Day 7

DADDY WAITED FOR A GOOD DAY, then sent me over to the seventy acres to burn the piles of mesquite. The waiting gave the cut sprouts time to dry out, to lose their sap, and the good day, this particular Saturday in November, was a wet one, on the heels of a norther that had pushed a line of drizzle as far south as East Texas where it stalled on its way to the Gulf Coast.

A frost had settled on the land the night before Halloween. As I drove the Ford over to the seventy acres, the deciduous trees, the sycamores and oaks and sweet gums that had been brash and bright with their yellows and oranges and reds now held only a thin scattering of brown curled leaves. The pecan trees had been bare of leaves for weeks, but still held black clusters of empty hulls, open with mute surprise against the sky. The pastures on either side of the highway had thinned, and were dotted with dirt-gray, short-cropped stubbles of grass.

I drove west alone, glancing back and forth from the speedometer to the side mirror of the car. The trunk was open, the lid raised high to accommodate a five-gallon can of diesel fuel, then pulled down tight and tied with a piece of clothesline rope. The fuel sloshed with the motion of the car, a rhythmic, restless tide.

The summer of mesquite cutting had stopped abruptly after my week on the seventy acres. Between mowing sessions and old-fence stretching, I had found time to get my "hardship" driver's license. With Sally and I both driving, Daddy had broken down and bought another car—a new black Buick that, I suspect, Mother had a hand in picking out.

With those two events—a driver's license and an extra car—I found my freedom, at least some version of freedom, and for the first month or so after becoming road-legal I volunteered to drive everywhere—run errands to the store, pick up this, pick up that. I didn't care as long as the wheels turned under me.

Nights I picked up a buddy, Ronnie or Stick or Satch, and we cruised from the courthouse square to the Dairy Queen out on the highway and back again, never tiring of the imagined possibilities of that two-mile round trip. If we finally got bored with the drive, I nosed the Ford in at the Dairy Queen, parking out front. We settled on the car's fenders and trunk, where nothing could escape us.

But there was a downside. Now I could drive over to wherever the tractor and mower had been left—to the seventy acres or, even worse, to the "Holiman Place," a bramble and bloodweed-ridden, overgrown pasture Daddy had bought in the Trinity River bottom. There I would end up mowing pastures, day after steamy day, trying to keep the tractor's leaky radiator from overheating, hoping I didn't get a flat tire.

Or like today, when the residue of those summer days working, all of that cutting and stacking of mesquite, had to be finished off with a burning. While I drove, I listened to KLIF out of Dallas, a top-40 station that had daytime power enough to reach to Athens. I fiddled with the dial when power lines set up a field of static, and fiddled with the windshield wipers to keep the drizzle wiped clean.

Fumes from the diesel fuel in the back wafted through the car. I rolled my window down when there was no traffic coming, and back up again when I met a car or a truck to avoid the highway spray. I sat up straight, leaning forward a little when I got to the Trinity River bridge. I had crossed it before, had even driven the tractor at its full speed of fifteen miles an hour across this narrow, two-lane span. But I hadn't driven it in the rain. I had to grip the steering wheel tight when the tire spray from an oncoming car momentarily blocked my vision. I spotted a cattle truck swaying down the hill towards me in the distance and hit the gas hard, the Ford roaring more than accelerating, but I beat the truck to the end of the bridge and safety.

When I pulled into Kerens I stopped at the Dairy Mart for a Dr Pepper, avoiding eye contact with an assortment of country boys who had gathered there. I pulled away, back onto the highway, peeling a hint of rubber when I hit second gear, and watching in the rearview mirror, hoping for some reaction. I imagined a chase, the boys at the Dairy Mart seeing me as a threat to the Kerens girls and taking off in their Chevy pickups after me. In my imagination I would hit third gear in a hurry (which I now did) and leave them far behind.

At the turnoff that led north to the seventy acres, I slowed. I knew the turn well, had taken that gravel road numerous times before, mostly riding with Daddy. But once I had crowded into a black sedan with five of my older Kerens' cousins, pallbearers for an uncle's funeral, and we made this identical turn on our way from the little church in town out to the Prairie Point cemetery. I don't remember much about the funeral, except the ride out and back in the long sedan, the six of us squirming in our clip-on ties and too-short-in-the-sleeves suit coats, the air heavy with after shave lotion and cigarette smoke.

But today as I slowed at that familiar turnoff, I almost came to a stop. I checked the fuel gauge, saw I had a half tank, and felt a strange urge not to turn north at all, but to keep going. Straight would lead me to Corsicana, where I could turn to the right and head towards Dallas, and then who knows where. A quick calculation—eight gallons of gas at twenty miles to the gallon—and I projected myself way out beyond Fort Worth into territory where I'd never been. I could only imagine it as black and red and blue roads on the state highway map.

Beyond Fort Worth. Just thinking about that sent a chill through me. I had a couple of dollars, emergency money Daddy had grudgingly handed me earlier—the two dollars not to be spent frivolously, but saved to fix a flat or buy a fan belt. And I had a little change of my own from the drink I'd bought at the Dairy Mart. Not enough for much of a trip, I decided. But the possibility of going on—just the thought itself—rushed through me.

The gravel surface of the road north provided good enough traction for a half-dozen miles, but the side road that led to the seventy acres was wet gumbo slick, the tires spinning and sliding between grabbing patches of gravel. On the slick spots I gunned the Ford, my blood racing with the whip of the car's rear end.

At the barbed wire gap that opened onto the seventy acres, the little herd of cows charged me, mooing, bawling, carrying on. I pulled through the gap and fastened it behind me and the cows sniffed the car, eager for a sack of range cubes or at least a bale of hay. I tried to spook them away with the horn, but they were horn-broke, had learned to come for cow-grub at the honk of the horn, and only jumped a little, not scared at all.

I eased the car across the matted needle grass to a place as near to my old campsite at the bois d'arc grove as I dared and stopped. I sat still, surveying the piles of mesquite before me while the diesel fuel gently sloshed and quieted behind me.

The stacks of mesquite seemed smaller than when I had cut them. They had settled, I figured, and had certainly lost their leaves, for now they were a tangle of thorny limbs. The rest of the mesquite still standing in the pasture looked smaller, more vulnerable, and I thought about cutting a few more while they were in that stage. The entire place seemed fragile, the hay shed bedraggled, its rusted tin roof dull in the overcast day. The fences seemed to sag more than before, and the tank dam in the distance was earth-bare and eroding.

It was all I could do to ease the can of diesel fuel to the ground. In a sack that mother had packed for me I rummaged around for the box of kitchen matches and found first—and finished off in four bites—a limp, frigid, waxed-paper-wrapped piece of apple pie meant to be my dessert. There were a couple of sandwiches for later, and a newspaper-insulated quart of sweetened iced tea. It would stay cold today.

In the back seat, Daddy had stuffed two burlap tow sacks to be soaked in the stock tank and used to beat the edges of the fire in case it started to spread. As wet as the grass was, and with a mist still in the air, I would ignore that. He had given me instructions, stuff I already knew: Splash the stacks of mesquite with the diesel fuel and set the can well back out of the way. Light the piles on the upwind side. Don't light more than two or three stacks of brush at a time. And wait for those to die down before you light two or three more.

"If you have a problem," Daddy said, "get Roy Clyde, he'll give you a hand." And then he stopped. He shot me his skeptical look. "You can handle this, I reckon?"

I gave him my best sure-I-can look and nodded.

"And I don't want to hear that you're racing that car all over the place, burning the engine up. Check the oil, watch the gauges. And watch those mesquite thorns. There's a spare in the trunk, but it's pretty slick."

"Yes, sir," I said. The thought of racing around, all over the place—maybe getting into trouble—did intrigue me. But how to accomplish that over here around the seventy acres, I couldn't imagine. Maybe Daddy knew something, had as a boy done something that I didn't know. Or maybe he was warning me not to get too big for my britches, for we had had a confrontation of sorts earlier in the summer, a week or two before I got my driver's license.

It had happened one Saturday morning when we hauled some salt blocks out to the pasture near Athens where he ran a few cows. I drove—"practice driving" for my upcoming driver's exam. Daddy sat beside me, impatiently drawing on his pipe, and focused hawklike on my every move. Mother rode in the back, sitting behind me to avoid the drift of pipe smoke. Her steady flow of words washed over me, the story (once again) of how my Aunt Dee Dee's roughneck husband had sold their house while she was laid up in the hospital with an appendectomy. Daddy grunted and I could tell that my Uncle Frank's gutsy independence secretly pleased him.

We carried a half-dozen salt blocks in the car's trunk—smooth, yellow, twenty-five pound cubes to be located on scrap pieces of tin in each of the open pastures.

I maneuvered the car around the cow trails, stopping here and there, waiting, one hand nonchalantly resting over the steering wheel while Daddy placed the blocks in some special way that he alone understood.

Finally only two of the salt blocks remained to be dropped off—on the far side of the draw that split the pasture in half. That required crossing the creek, which could be tricky. First, there was the descent down a rutted incline, keeping the wheels of the car on the high ridges so not to drag high center. Then, at just the right moment, you had to hit the gas hard in order to roar across the clay-slip of the creek bottom and make it safely up the opposite side.

I pulled the car to the edge of the draw in order to survey the route. It had rained the day before and a little water still stood in the bottom of the creek. I hesitated, studied the glistening red clay, gazed at the open field beyond. Daddy impatiently motioned me on, biting hard on his pipe. I eased down the slope, managed to keep the tires out of the deepest ruts. When I neared the bottom, Daddy hollered, "Now, gun it! Gun it!" and I did, hitting the gas, popping back the clutch. The Ford lurched forward. The engine died. The car sank, and I did, too.

Daddy groaned. I hit the starter again and gunned the engine, but we had lost momentum, and the tires spun, rim deep in the mud.

"Dadgummit," Daddy hollered, "I told you to gun it." He jerked open his door and stepped out into the red bog. "You can't cross this creek unless you hit it hard. I told you that, and you just eased it down. Dadgummit!"

"Now, Daddy," Mother said from the back seat and patted me on the shoulder.

I got out, checked how far the tires had sunk. "Maybe I can try again, get some traction."

"Too late for traction. When I say gun it, you've got to really gun it. You can't pussyfoot a car across this creek!"

From somewhere, a place, I suppose, that had been growing secretly inside of me, came a voice I hardly recognized as my own. "You can't talk to me that way," I said. My voice rang strong, but my insides trembled.

Daddy stopped his stewing, looked at me for a minute. "I'll get the tractor," he finally said, and stomped up the incline and across the pasture towards the barn.

That incident had left me apprehensive. It had seemed to clear the air for a while, but not for long. I was still the boy—something I knew, but hated to acknowledge—and he was the man.

Now I tossed the tow sacks from the backseat to the ground. There was no way I would trudge half way across the seventy acres to wet them down in that stink hole of a stock tank. Daddy wasn't here to tell me what to do, and besides, any fool could see that nothing would burn out here. Not today. I had my axe and a long-handled hoe to keep the fire under control. I knew what I was doing.

The hardest part, at first, was toting the diesel fuel around. I used a quart canning jar, filling it from the can, splashing it generously over the stacks of mesquite. A lot of walking back and forth until the can got light enough to easily carry. I shed my junior-high letter jacket and tossed it to one side. The fuel oil chased a couple of rats from their nests—I thought about the rabbit from the summer, and kept my eye peeled, hoping to spot a three-legged cotton tail.

The fire caught in a quick roar, racing through the stacks, yellow and blue flames skittering, dancing from limb to limb. But after the first flash, the fire died down, leaving a few blackened, smoldering limbs.

"Well, shit," I said out loud, and started the process again. There were fifteen or more stacks that reached head high, and it was slow going to soak all of the stacks once more. But I did, finally emptying out the last of the five gallon can. If this doesn't work, I thought, then these piles won't ever burn.

But a worry ran through me, and while I moved from stack to stack, relighting the fires, I rehearsed what I would tell Daddy if I couldn't get the mesquite to burn. I could see his look, feel his disapproval and disgust at my ineptitude. Reasons and then excuses raced through my head as I went over how I would explain myself. The possibilities ranged from the plausible to the outlandish, from the truth to the fudging of the truth: The mesquite was still too green. The ground around the stacks was too wet. A big rain started just as I lit the stacks and it doused the fires. I was afraid that the flames would scare the cows.

About that time the stacks caught, all fifteen of them, and all at once. The flames soared skyward, carrying blackened bits of ash and sparks. Limbs and branches snapped and sizzled and then collapsed from the intense heat. I backed off and watched, holding the hoe ready at my side.

Now my worry changed. What if Daddy had been right? What if I should have lit only two or three stacks at a time? For the flames began to edge out into the needle grass, the straw-dry grass sparking and flaring and falling in black strands to the ground.

It didn't take long for me to identify the problem, one I hadn't anticipated. The heat of the fire was drying out the grass all around the stacks, and the hotter the stacks burned the more grass dried out, and the greater the blackened circle became.

"Holy shit," I yelled and attacked the flames with the hoe, scraping the dirt at the blackened edge of one fire, but that proved practically worthless. After only a couple of minutes the heat drove me back. I ran to the car for the tow sacks. I started to drive to the stock tank, but figured the car would bog down between here and there. And if it bogged down (and the horror of that thought almost sank me to my knees), the flames might take the car. The consequences of that were too painful to imagine, so I took off running, the tow sacks trailing a stream of golden dust behind me.

At the stock tank I glanced back at the piles of brush, now glowing, throbbing from the heat. The whole seventy acres seemed about to go up in flames. I eased to the edge of the tank, mud covering the tops of my tennis shoes, and slapped the sacks across the surface of murky water. But they wouldn't sink, and wouldn't absorb the water. Finally I threw a giant rock onto one of them. It sank and I waded ankle deep to retrieve it, and sank the other one.

By this time I was sweating, but I could hardly feel my half-frozen feet. I raced back with the dripping sacks and began to beat at the edges of the flames. The tow sacks were heavy now—when they thumped across the burning grass showers of soot and ash and sparks swirled around me. My feet were no longer cold, but hot, and I could smell the burning rubber of my scorched tennis shoes.

I thought again of the highway that led west, out somewhere past Fort Worth, and figured that might still be a possibility. Maybe a necessity. But Fort Worth and beyond no longer really appealed to me. I hoped that somehow Daddy would drive up and help me, and at the same time prayed that he wouldn't catch me in such a fix.

Then someone was beside me, jolting me back to the heat and the flames in the pasture. It was Roy Clyde Jenkins, dragging a hose from the back of a wagon he trailered behind his pickup. The hose was connected to a huge water tank.

Roy Clyde nodded and grinned. Then he hit a switch and a generator popped on, and then the water shot out, not a big stream, but big enough, I figured.

While Roy Clyde worked the hose I attacked the blackened edges with new energy. In only a few minutes the fires began to burn themselves out and the mesquite stacks crumpled and settled, now hardly more than low mounds of ash and glowing coals. I moved around, tossing and kicking stray half-burned ends of mesquite limbs into the piles where they flamed up and then blackened.

"Think you can handle it now?" Roy Clyde asked.

I nodded.

Roy Clyde grinned. He was a small man with wavy black

hair. His voice was steady, calm, as if this sort of thing happened every day. "Good thing I was home, I reckon. I keep this old wagon around in case my barn catches or something. Only used it a couple of times in twenty years."

I told him thanks, thanks a lot. And he nodded then—while he rolled up the hose—like it was no big deal. "Your daddy's helped me out before," he said. "Payback time, I reckon. What neighbors are for."

The impatient honking of a car at the gap to the seventy acres turned us around.

"Hell, it's James Lee," Roy Clyde said, giving a nod in the direction of the car. "Maybe you better get that gate for him." He turned back to winding up the hose.

I moved easily across the pasture, headed for Uncle James who, I knew, would be antsy waiting in his car. My arms and T-shirt and jeans were heavy with wet ash and grit. My white tennis shoes, long since the color of dirt, were heavy with ash-black mud. But relief overwhelmed me, relief that it wasn't Daddy who had driven up right then, relief that I hadn't burned the whole seventy acres, and the Ford, my freedom car, with it. Even relief, at least for now, that I wasn't somewhere out beyond Fort Worth, broke and running low on gas.

Uncle James was Daddy's brother, younger by more than twenty years. He had been struck down with polio at twelve. Now, in his late twenties, braces ran the length of both his withered legs. He click-locked the braces straight so he could stand and get around with his crutches, but getting in and out of the car was a slow process for him. He often recruited me to go along when he needed some help. The 1952 Chevy that he drove was rigged with hand levers for the accelerator and brake pedal and clutch, and Uncle James drove that car with a flurry of hand movements that amazed me.

He had been over to his pasture, I guessed, checking on his half-dozen cows, tossing them some range cubes from a sack he kept in the car. His few acres were farther to the east, maybe seven or eight dirt-road miles from the seventy acres where I worked. They joined twenty-four rock-littered acres that my Grand-dad Watt owned. Together the two places of less than fifty acres must have made up the sorriest piece of ground in the county. They were situated at the crest of a hill, the last high place before the road fell quickly down towards the Trinity River bottom where it petered out among native pecan trees and cockleburrs and blood-weeds in my Uncle Russell Baxter's pasture.

Grand-dad and Granny Watt lived in town, in Kerens. Only a rambling sweetheart rose bush and the hand-formed brick from a now caved-in dug well marked their old home place. Daddy had salvaged some of the lumber for our house in Athens, and later burned the rest of that bare-bones, three-room structure. Mother took a cutting from the rose bush, and when it rooted, planted it in a bed outside the kitchen of our house where it still blossoms every summer.

Daddy used Grand-dad's twenty-four acres for fall pasture—when Uncle James didn't use it—although it would carry his dozen cows no more than a few weeks until they grazed the grass short. But it gave the seventy acres a chance at rejuvenation if we were lucky and got a couple of decent rains.

Moving the cows from Daddy's seventy acres to Grand-dad's place, however, was problematic. The seventy acres had no loading chute. This presented no difficulty when Daddy bought a cow and calf at the Friday auction and paid some cowboy—"Pig" Westbrook, more times than not—to haul them to his pasture. Pig just backed his trailer towards a shallow wash until the twin wheels dropped low enough for the cow and her baby to skitter safely out the trailer's back end.

But moving the entire herd from the seventy acres to Granddad's place—maybe twenty head of cows, calves and a strong-headed bull—presented another challenge. Hauling cattle out of there without a catch pen or a corral was next to impossible. Even in the best of circumstances it would have taken Pig Westbrook, with his two cow dogs and a horse, most of a day and a couple of round trips in his trailer. That would not have come cheap.

Daddy's solution was to drive his little herd the eight miles down the dirt road between pastures. The technique was for Mother to lead the way in the car, the Ford's trunk propped open, exposing a broken bundle of hay and a half-sack of range cubes.

So Mother took off, honking the Ford's horn. Dick watched the action from the backseat of the car. I trotted along one side of the little herd, and Sally half-heartedly worked the other side. Daddy, wielding a rotted-end fence post, brought up the rear. It was his job to keep the cows from dallying along and munching on mouthfuls of roadside greenery when they got discouraged because they couldn't catch up to the bale of hay in the trunk of the car.

This cattle drive took three or four hours, most of the way pretty smooth, with Daddy only occasionally hollering at Mother, "Talkie, slow it down," or "Talkie, dadgummit, keep it moving!" Mother, grinding gears, muttered to herself, and glared back at Daddy in the rearview mirror.

Most of the way we had barbed wire fences on both sides of the road, but when we got around Bazette, fenced fields gave way to a few houses, and the cows shot off to the right and to the left, into front yards and vegetable gardens. They topped irises and rose bushes and tromped down all sorts of treasured growing things.

"Keep those blame cows in the road," Daddy would holler, and I sprinted ahead in a sorry attempt to head off some flower bed destruction. From the safety of their front porches, and with frowns of disapproval, women—all of them some-odd removed kin on one side of our family or the other—shooed the cows with dish towels and flapping aprons.

We finally approached Grand-dad's place, foot-sore and frustrated, Daddy reduced from yelling to more all-inclusive and general grumbling. Now it was up to me to race ahead of the herd, sidestepping cows and cow patties, and get the barbed wire gate open so Mother could, in one last dash, and honking the horn for all it was worth, gun the Ford up an incline and finally to a stop in the middle of the pasture—where the cows were supposed to follow.

But I guess by then the cows had moved beyond being horn-broke and become road-broke, more interested in roadside grazing than in that bale of dried-out hay in the trunk of the car. I armed myself with a stout cedar pole and did my best to turn them in the gate, but the little herd kept on coming, scrambling around me, bawling after I popped them across their bony rumps when they bolted past me, and headed on down the road.

When Daddy caught up, he threw his hat to the road in disgust. "Dadgummit, Donnie," he hollered, but I was gone, sprinting past the startled cows, until I found a place I could contain them for a try at a U-turn. We had cows, but we sure weren't cowboys.

SOMETIMES, IN THE EARLY FALL, I would meet my Uncle James on the twenty-four acres a few Saturdays during dove-hunting season. When we hunted doves, Uncle James would pull his Chevy down past a grove of trees fifty feet behind the dam of a muddy dug tank. This tank was no more than the easy toss of a rock across, but in a dry fall when water was scarce—and there were several of those seasons in the mid-to-late fifties—doves would circle in to water right at dusk.

It was my job to get Uncle James down next to the tank, where we both half-hid underneath the leafy spread of a lone willow tree. To do this I carried my uncle across that stone-cobbled ground, struggling not to stumble, not to lose my grip, not to drop him, for Daddy had warned me of the consequences—probably leg amputation—if James ever fell and broke a major bone.

After I settled him onto the bottom slope of the dam, it was back to the car for his gun and shells and a mason jar of water and his cigarettes, which he always forgot.

I had bought an Ithaca twelve-gauge pump the summer before from Spencer Hardware in Athens, paying it out by the week with money I earned mowing neighbors' yards and working odd jobs here and there. I loved that gun, the smoothness of the blue-black barrel, the precision with which smooth-coated shells snapped up and in its metallic underbelly, the blast, and then the kick against my shoulder, the lingering odor of gunpowder.

That fall, I knelt by my Uncle James on the hid-side of that tank and we blasted the air full of #6 pellets, and even dropped a few doves.

At dark we drove back into Kerens. My Watt grandparents—Granny and Grand-dad, we called them—lived next to the high school football field in a turn-of-the-century, two-story house set back in a grove of pecan trees. The bones of the house were lovely, but the wood siding was paint-weathered off-gray, and the house sagged so much in the middle that when you moved from room to room you had to touch a chair or a doorframe to steady yourself. Off to one side of the house a couple of chicken houses held hundreds of laying hens that provided Granny and Grand-dad with what little income they had.

Until they died, the house never had running hot water or air conditioning. Bare light bulbs hung from long twisted cords in the center of every room, casting harsh shadows across the drab walls.

Uncle James lived in Waco, where he taught and counseled and administered tests for schools and various government agencies. With the help of Daddy's monthly check, sent with generosity and difficulty and some resentment, James had a few years before earned his master's degree at the University of Texas. Finally he was on his own, as independent as a man in his situation could be. He drove the hour and a half back to Kerens most weekends—for a couple of reasons, I later figured.

He obviously was lonely living in Waco by himself, and found comfort in his mother and dad. He got a kick from driving out to the few acres he had bought near Bazette and checking on his cows.

There were a couple of old friends he had gone to high school with still around Kerens. One of them was Roy Clyde, who, in the burning of the seventy acres, had proved himself to be a solid fellow. But one of James' friends ended up operating the only pharmacy in town—a high-ceilinged, red-brick store on the main street of mostly abandoned buildings. When I drove over to Kerens to work at the seventy acres or to hunt, and circled through town to check out the action (which I never discovered, probably because there was none), I found James there, parked out front more than once, his pharmacist friend leaning on the door of the Chevy. The two of them acted strangely when I pulled up next to them, overly cheerful, overly nice, the way a kid acts when he's trying too hard to act naturally.

I might be wrong, but I figured that Uncle James found comfort from the pain of his life from behind the counter of that drug store. In later years, I got midnight, slurred-talk phone calls from him. Sometimes he was euphoric, sometimes depressed, his mood swings metered by booze, most certainly, and by other, more complex prescriptions, I suspect.

Daddy had a hard time with Uncle James, could barely conceal his impatience when his little brother started in on his university-tainted way of talking, a holding forth of sorts that would get Daddy up and pacing before he bolted the room.

Daddy always resented college boys, whether engineers and geologists from California—green recruits at Standard Oil in Houston—or big-shot, small-town lawyers in Athens.

But despite his conflicted feelings, he mostly supported James through the university, as earlier he had helped his sister get her degree in math so that she could teach high school for the next forty years.

It had been dark when Uncle James and I pulled up out front of Grand-dad's house after our afternoon of hunting. I toted the collapsed wheel chair from his car and left it opened up on the front porch. While James made his way up the rough-brick front walk on his crutches, I gripped the back of his belt with one hand. He worked his way up the front three steps to the porch where I helped him ease into the wheelchair.

Granny stood just inside the screen door and watched, wiping—or wringing—her hands on a kitchen towel. Granny was a worrier—I guess there had always been plenty to worry about. And James was both the beneficiary and victim of her anxiety.

Grand-dad, a slight man with thinning hair and splotchy skin, was the quietist man I ever knew. He nodded from across the room when I pulled the door open and James rolled in. Grand-dad rose out of his chair—a gesture it seemed, an ineffectual offer to be of help in some way. Then he eased back down in his chair, listening while Granny fussed over James and scurried back to the kitchen where supper had been waiting on the 1920s vintage stove for hours.

We gathered at a table of some dark and dull wood covered with a crocheted tablecloth. Around a platter of fried chicken—always chicken—we bowed our heads while Grand-dad mumbled a prayer, the same prayer I had listened to scores of times. I never understood a word of the prayer, but it was the same, I could tell, by its brevity and the flatness of its intonations. Grand-dad was an elder in the tiny Church of Christ that met in the no-frills, white frame building just up the street. But his beliefs were muted, and at home, except for his perfunctory prayer, religion didn't seem to intrude in his life.

James carried the conversation while we ate, with nervous, self-conscious talk that held forth, filled the silence of the room in a decent sort of way, one that I was grateful for. He was a handsome man, took pride in being a sharp dresser, was proud of his black wavy hair that he combed straight back. His upper body, above his useless legs, was stout and muscular. He possessed an alert and lively intellect.

In a few years Uncle James would meet and marry a woman whose only fault in Mother's eyes was being from Boston, and being Catholic—something the poor woman could never overcome. We drove over to Waco for the wedding on a windy Saturday one fall, and on out into the country to a small and isolated Catholic church that had been sited on the only hill for miles around. These were still the Latin days of that religion, and my first time in a Catholic church. The ceremony was full-blown traditional with incense and holy water and organ music and a richly-robed priest—all off-limits in the Church of Christ.

Afterwards, we made our way back out of the church to the open air where we stood around mostly strangers and waited for the bride and groom to appear. I spotted Daddy at the edge of the gathering, lighting a cigarette. I moved out next to him, uncomfortable in the noose of my thin tie, ready to get on back home.

From where we stood you could see for miles across that country, a bleak landscape of picked-out cotton fields and weed-ridden pastures dotted with a scattering of farm houses. We stood there a minute, silent, ignoring the hubbub behind us. Daddy checked over his shoulder, to make sure we were alone. "Well," he said, "I reckon they got married." And he shook his head in disbelief.

NOW, BACK AT THE SEVENTY ACRES, as I approached Uncle James' car, he motioned past me, waving his arm out towards the scorched pasture. "Looks like you tried to burn off the whole place," he said. He gave a little grin, shook his head.

I didn't answer, dragged the barbed wire gate open. James drove through and I closed it behind him. He motioned for me to get in, so I pushed the sack of range cubes to one side and slid in beside him.

"I cut that danged mesquite all one week," I told him. "Back in June. Daddy said now was a good time for burning."

James snorted. "Well, it sure was a good time for burning, it looks like. Yeah, I'd seen what you cut. Wondered when your daddy would get around to cleaning the mess up."

James drove slowly across the field, easing around the mesquite stumps and stobs of the cut-over mesquite, pulling in next to Roy Clyde's pickup.

I slipped out of his car, left the old friends to talk. They were grinning, watching me walk away. I didn't want to hear what they would say about the way I let the fire get the best of me. So I gathered up my tools, and found my letter jacket, and decided it was time for the ham sandwiches and jug of tea.

While I ate I looked out over the pasture. Now there was a

considerable clearing before me. Sure, a bunch of the grass was blackened, but it would come back in the spring. Daddy would figure out what had happened when he saw the place, or probably Uncle James would tell him.

To Uncle James and Roy Clyde it would make a good story, a funny commentary on me, the way fourteen-year-old boys mess up. But Daddy wouldn't laugh, I knew, would hold it against me, and I could hear him now, the way he would say "Dadgummit, Donnie, you could have burned the fences down," and on and on. He might even throw his hat—if he was wearing an old one—to the ground.

He would tell Mother, I knew, but she wouldn't say anything to me, just be distant for a few days, not look me right in the eye. She would leave the room, or get busy with something of little consequence when I came around.

Some of the mesquite I had cut might sprout back in the spring, and the grass and the weeds would emerge from their roots to green the charred ground. Rains would wash the ash, pound it, dissolve it back into the earth. The winds would dry and scatter what was left, and the land would be healed.

I gazed out on the land and saw all of that, felt all of those things, and knew that none of it much mattered. What did matter were the seven days I had worked. It mattered that I could see what I had accomplished, even if it wasn't done quite right, even if it didn't last. It mattered that with my hands and my strength and my determination I had finished the work.

It mattered most of all that the Ford was safe, that when I slid into the seat the engine fired up, and that I pulled away, headed towards the gate, past Roy Clyde and my Uncle James who would wonder why I didn't stop to talk, why I kept on going, moving past them with a slight nod and a confident lift of my hand.

Haley,
Texas
1959

Haley, Texas 1959 is a work of fiction, but like all such fictions this story has its origin in memory. In the writing of *Seven Days Working*, a particular incident surfaced which I recorded, but could not quite forget. The remembrance stayed in my subconscious, until over time the meanderings of my mind had embellished, distorted, and finally replaced the original incident. The only truths that remain in this story are the shadowed glimpses of place, the remnants of voices, and my intuitive sense of suppressed pain. The rest of the story is a result of my imagination.

—Donley Watt

Chapter 1

WHAT DAMON REMEMBERED most clearly from that Sunday night was the two-by-four—cracked and splintered at one end—a ten-foot length of yellow pine board, splattered with lighter fluid and burning, the flames skating blue and yellow across the board's surface, the smoke and fumes blending into the stench that always drifted across the county dump.

The four boys stood on that rubbled ground, watching without speaking. Farris, the oldest of the boys, flipped the two-by-four once with the toe of his boot, making certain that the flames charred the blood-splattered end of the board. Then they left, the boys scrambling, sliding across the seats of Farris' 1955 Chevy, Royce and Billy Ray in the back, and Damon once again in the front passenger seat—his cousin Farris hitting the starter a couple of times unsuccessfully, then waiting an interminable few seconds before trying it again.

In that gap of time, those few seconds between the dry grind of the starter and the roar of the engine when the timing and the gasoline and the spark all co-joined, in those seconds of waiting, Billy Ray whispered "Shit" as if shit were a barely audible prayer and not a curse at all, and Royce pounded on the back of Damon's seat, his fists slamming against the padded vinyl in frustration as he moaned, "Start, you son of a bitch! Start!"

Farris guided his Chevy back out the way he had driven in, the car lights off, easing past the pushed-up mounds of garbage and dozer-dug pits and piles of brush. A layer of putrid air hung over them, seeping through the rolled-tight windows. Damon breathed through his open mouth, dog-like, his breaths shallow and grudging.

Even at night, even now in the frost-bite of late December, swarms of garbage-fattened, green-winged flies pinged against the car, looping in arcs like crazed dive-bombers. Farris leaned forward, high over the steering wheel, straining to see, but guiding the car more by feel than by sight, the tires finding their own way in the slick ruts that curved back to the main road.

There Farris hesitated a moment. Then, without a word, he whipped the Chevy to the right, to the south, away from Haley, the town that was home to the four of them. The car fishtailed, the tires spinning off globs of black mud, before Farris straightened it out on the asphalt road. He jerked the lights on and stomped them bright, and in a moment floorboarded the accelerator, the twin mufflers giving off their mellifluous blats until the car reached seventy and began to shimmy. Farris eased the car back down to sixty and held it there, steady, looking neither to his right—where on the periphery of vision a dark line of pecan trees followed the meanderings of Dead Dog Creek—nor to his left across the flat-stretched land, dark-ribboned with monotonous, spare lines of turned-under rows of cotton.

In the back seat Billy Ray began to laugh, an odd and inappropriate laugh—one of those uncontrollable laughs that Damon understood. It was the same kind of laugh that he used to get at church when he was younger, six or seven, when he and a little friend would do no more than exchange glances and—for no reason at all—break out into shaking, gasping laughter. They tried to stifle it, but never could until his daddy in his robes behind the oak pulpit would pause in the middle of his Sunday sermon, pause for what seemed forever, and stare at them, waiting, the stare an unspoken threat of incomprehensible after-church punishment if they didn't stop. The stare was directed also at Iris—his wife and Damon's mother. It accused her, specifically blaming her for not controlling their son. That was the kind of laughter erupting from Billy Ray, a high-pitched and chest-aching laughter without apparent reason or foreseeable end.

Damon remembered a family story that his mother told. Although Damon's daddy was the preacher, Iris Wilson told the stories. One of her favorites—this happened before Damon was born, or at least before he had acquired a conscious memory—related how one of her Uncle Robert's boys, a first cousin of hers and a grown man, had laughed uncontrollably at his own mother's funeral. Finally he had to stagger from the church, make his way to the front door for fresh air, gasping and wheezing his way past his solemn and disapproving kin.

Now Billy Ray, with a deep-catch stutter-breath, got quiet. He tried to flex his hand, make a fist. "Son of a bitch," he muttered. "Broke the son of a bitch." Billy Ray was a big-headed boy with a thick shag of orange-red hair that he kept closely clipped. His eyes set back into his big head—as if his head had swollen and engulfed them almost completely, leaving him to peer out at the world in a furtive, suspicious manner. Billy Ray found those slit-eyes with his uninjured hand, and wiped at them, wiped the stream of laughter-tears from his face with the freckled back of that left hand.

Earlier that evening Billy Ray had sat behind Farris, just the way he sat now. He had grasped one end of that two-by-four, had braced it, pushed it hard against the back of the driver's seat so that its length cocked up and some five feet out the open window on Royce's side.

But still Billy Ray had not been ready when the end of the board struck Willie Lee Brown and knocked him prostrate to the slick-clay edge of the road's shoulder. There had been a crack. Damon remembered that. A crack that he heard above the sound of the wind that sliced through the open rear window, above the blat-blat-blat of the twin mufflers as the Chevy slowed. A crack and a thud. The sounds so close together—*crackthud*—that Damon had no way of knowing what had happened, or which sound had come first.

The crack may have been the two-by-four, for when it collided with Willie Lee Brown it gave and split and splintered. Or the crack, the sound that Damon heard, may have been the crunch and shatter of vertebrae, when the bones of Willie Lee Brown's neck dry-limb snapped from the force of the sap-rich board.

Or the crack could have been Billy Ray's wrist bone, but wasn't, for Damon had broken his own arm two years before at Slater's Skating Rink, and he hadn't heard a bone-snapping sound at all. The crack was not the bone in Billy Ray's wrist, even if it did break, even, as Billy Ray had claimed, he wasn't ready for the shock, didn't have a tight grip on the board.

Billy Ray's not being ready understandable, for in all the times that the three older boys—Farris and Billy Ray and Royce—had gone nigger knockin', they had never even gotten close to striking a colored man. So Billy Ray could have only imagined and projected the jolt and wrench of the board as it slammed against a body. The colored men who walked that lonely road at night had always before been alert to white men's cars, and always before retreated, hopping across the weed-ridden bar ditch when a car behind them slowed and eased to the edge of the road, the tires pinging loose gravel up in the fender wells in warning.

The thud of the simultaneous crackthud had been the weight of the board as exerted against the weight of Willie Lee Brown, the force of a yellow pine two-by-four traveling at forty miles an hour colliding with the hardly moving mass of a man.

They had lifted the two-by-four from a construction site in town that very night—the one at the First Methodist Church where Damon's father preached twice on Sundays, had preached earlier this very evening, the board wedged into a tight stack of lumber at the site of a new educational wing that the Reverend Wallace Wilson had for interminable Sundays exhorted the strapped congregation to fund and build.

Billy Ray had taken the two-by-four from the side of the church yard, but it was Farris who first said, "Let's go nigger knockin'." Farris looked over at Damon then, not a glance, but a questioning look, because Damon was younger than the rest of them. And Damon was the preacher's boy.

Damon remembered that look, had felt it before, the questioning without words, the way other eyes—and now his cousin Farris' eyes—had sought out some inner truth in him. Damon knew this was his opportunity to back out—the moment to shake his head no—and for Farris to drop him back at Aunt Nell's house where his daddy and mama would still be.

Are you man enough for this? Farris' eyes asked. "Sissy" and "coward" and "chicken" and "preacher's boy" and all sorts of other words like that raced through Damon's mind. "Preacher's boy" was the worst. He hated being the preacher's boy. Why couldn't his daddy drive a truck or own the drug store or work in the bank? *Are you man enough for this?* Farris' eyes asked.

And in response Damon had shrugged. Then he nodded.

Just stared straight ahead and shrugged and nodded.

Now on the flat asphalt road south of town—south of the county dump where the charred two-by-four still flamed and blackened—Royce shifted forward in the back seat. Damon could feel the boy's closeness, could smell the butch wax of his flat top. "Where we headed?" he asked, the question aimed at Farris, the words going right by Damon who at twelve was the youngest of the four boys by three or four years. "What in the hell we gonna do?" he whined.

"When we hit the creek road in a couple of miles..." Farris said, "…at Southtown…" He stopped mid-sentence and gave an ironic sound then, not quite a laugh, but a guttural sound that followed the words which had come out calm and even, flat as the flatness of the plowed-under cotton land they raced across, as calm as if the four of them had been on their way out to Dead Dog Creek to check some shiner-baited throw lines. "...at Southtown we'll hang a right and ease into Corsicana from there, hang around the Dairy Mart for a while. Be loud, be seen. There'll be lots of witnesses." Farris gave a little laugh then, as if he had held it in before and now let it escape into the car's stale air. He turned his head to one side and Damon could make out the acne craters and pits on his face, the stubble of his buzzed-close hair.

Farris shifted a wad of tobacco from one cheek to the other as if he were making room for the words that followed. The voice was not his own at all, but that of a different person. "Where you boys been this late?" Farris' voice was a deep drawl. Then he shifted the tobacco back and his voice changed too, changed into a higher version of his own voice. "Why, Mr. High Sheriff, we've been nooky-chasing in Corsicana all night."

"What about my wrist?" Billy Ray whimpered. "I got a broke wrist. I need a doctor, a X-ray, maybe a cast."

Farris thought a minute. He looked over at Damon. "You

okay?" he asked. "I don't have to tell you what to do, what to say, do I?"

Damon shook his head—too quickly, he figured after he had done it, for he hadn't absorbed the violence of the night, had not taken into himself what they had done. Farris pointed ahead, as if he were projecting not down the desolate road, but into the near future. "Billy Ray, old buddy," he said, "you're fixing to get in a fight."

"Cut that crap out," Billy Ray shot back, "I can't move my damned arm, much less get in a mother fuckin' fight."

"Well, you will tonight. Somehow. Insult some Corsicana girl, a looker, ask her if she'll suck your dodie for a cream-a sodie. Make sure her boyfriend hears you. Then take one swing. That's all you need. Just land one blow with that bad hand, and we'll drag you off to some doctor."

"Oh, man," Billy Ray complained.

"Cut the crap," Farris says. "You're in trouble. Hell, we're all high-boot-deep in shit if we don't play this smart."

"What about cuz?" Royce said from behind. Damon could feel the boy's skinny finger punching through the padding of the seat, pushing at his back. "Can you trust your little cousin not to squeal? Not to be a baby?"

Damon stared straight ahead. He rolled the window down just a crack, sucked in some of the heavy December air.

"It's his ass, too," Farris said, shooting Damon a quick glance. "You thirteen now?"

"In May," Damon said.

"Shit," Royce said, "A goddamned baby."

"Shut that fucking pneumonia hole," Billy Ray complained, and Damon rolled the window up tight.

Farris slowed the car at a stop sign. The main road turned right, but to their left a rutted dirt road led past a random assemblage of houses that made up Southtown. One of the houses, Damon figured, was home for the colored man they had struck down, for the six-mile road between all-white Haley and all-black Southtown was the way back and forth to Tyner's Store at the south edge of Haley, the only store around that allowed colored folks to use the front door, the only store around that would let colored folks actually sign a tab for groceries and pay it off at the end of the month.

The boys looked to the left through a fine mist that hung suspended in the air. Damon could feel the other boys straining to see into the dark, but he could not know their thoughts, whether they felt remorse or satisfaction or confusion or fright. He could just make out the dilapidated school, a weathered gray-plank building that sagged in the middle, its dull tin roof. There weren't more than fifty students in all who went there, he figured, but still he dreaded when that school would shut down and the Southtown kids would be bused in to integrate the white schools in Haley.

The colored kids might be okay, but Damon knew there would be trouble, and knew his daddy would get in the middle of it somehow, most certainly on the side of the coloreds. Then Damon would be not only "preacher's boy," but the "nigger-lovin' preacher's boy."

He spotted Southtown's only church, where a single, bare bulb illuminated the A.M.E. Church sign out front. Damon had been in that church one special Sunday afternoon, with his daddy. On the drive out to that church Wallace Wilson had emphasized to Damon that his trip south of town was not to "keep the negroes in their places," as some white folks wanted, but "to offer support in these difficult times, to help them understand what Jesus Christ might have done, what Jesus Christ would expect of them. No more and no less."

The Reverend Wilson often used Damon as a mock audience

of one, trying out his language, trying out his logic, even trying out the generous timbre of his voice on his son. For the Reverend Wallace Wilson took his job as pastor seriously, even if his Methodist Church in Haley was second to the First Baptist Church, and even if his regular congregants numbered no more than sixty of the town's tiny population.

Of that summer afternoon in the Southtown A.M.E. church, Damon remembered most the heat, the flurry of hand-held, funeral-home-furnished fans in the dark hands of the women. A sad-eyed, long-haired, white-robed Jesus on one side of the fans, and "For Your Comfort, Compliments of Reed Brothers Mortuary"—a black funeral home in Corsicana—on the back.

But there was little comfort in the church that afternoon, rather an undercurrent of hostility that burst forth in fulmination and in the menace of prayers to a vengeful God, the prayers rising and falling over some incident that had occurred in the Plaquemine Parish jail over in Louisiana the week before.

That's hundreds of miles away, in a totally different world, Damon had thought at the time, and that thought made him impatient with his daddy, and impatient with the swarm and murmur of the colored folks gathered in the church.

The gathering in the Southtown church was followed by some shootings—the late-night peppering of a couple of Southtown houses—a light scattering of bird shot dinging the tin roofs, nothing serious enough to make the Corsicana paper, shotgun pellets apparently not aimed to do real harm. But for good reason it riled the community into protest.

All hell would break out now when the colored man's body was found by the side of the road. Damon's daddy would almost surely go back out to the Southtown church in an attempt to calm the community, to mollify their fears. "This time I won't go," Damon whispered softly. "He can't make me go." He felt tears in his eyes and looked the other way—away from his cousin—and watched his own sad reflection in the car window as the car idled for that protracted moment at the stop sign.

Then with a soft rumble from the mufflers, Farris turned right and gunned the car to the northwest, up the road where the lights of Corsicana blinked and glowed through the mist. Damon wanted to go home. He wished Farris would drop him by his house out north of Haley, and tonight could be a night the same as last night, when his daddy watched "The Honeymooners." For Wallace Wilson didn't miss that show on Saturday nights. Mother hadn't joined her husband in the living room to watch last night, was too busy stirring up some bran muffin batter to refrigerate over night and ladle into tins the next morning.

Wallace had said, "Mother, you're going to miss 'The Honeymooners,'" the saying by now a habit of saying, and not an urging for her to join him at all. Wallace Wilson knew his wife would not settle in next to him on the green and red plaid sofa. He had stopped expecting it, but still asked.

Iris did want to see "The Honeymooners," loved seeing how those strange New Yorkers lived, drawing consolation in the bumbling buffoonery and idiocy of Art Carney and Jackie Gleason—bumbling buffoonery and idiocy universal male traits, Iris now believed.

She had watched, moving surreptitiously back and forth from the kitchen, stopping for a few moments at a time, framed by the doorway, silently taking in the antics on the black and white screen. The flash of light illuminated the wide center part of her hair and the whiteness of her skin. She was a big-boned woman, large, but not heavy, with a no-nonsense demeanor that she didn't try to hide with fluff. She was no beauty and knew it, but was middle-of-the-road attractive, and seemed to accept her looks in a matter-of-fact way. She watched from the doorway to the kitchen with a cup towel folded across one arm, as if she were a waiter in a Dallas restaurant. Sometimes she smiled—Damon had seen her smile—whenever the audience and then Wallace gave out a roar of a laugh.

DAMON AND HIS PARENTS had earlier that evening gone over to Aunt Nell's and Uncle Floyd's for after-church supper, a pre-Christmas gathering the same as last year, where Aunt Nell brought out flat Pyrex pans of chicken spaghetti covered with melted cheese and a basket of brown-and-serve rolls and a platter covered with circles of syrupy sweet pineapple slices with a cube of cream cheese and a maraschino cherry topping each one.

After supper Damon's mother and Aunt Nell cleared the table, Iris Wilson borrowing one of her sister-in-law's aprons to protect her Sunday-night church dress. In a little while Damon heard kitchen sounds—the clatter of dishes, and water running into a dishpan of suds. Then a few minutes later he could make out Aunt Nell' snasal voice complaining, disapproving. He figured it was about her younger brother Frank who couldn't seem to keep his oil field roughneck job.

Damon wandered into the front room where the Reverend Wallace Wilson had sunk back into one of Uncle Floyd's twin recliners. Floyd Wyrick was Iris' oldest brother, a rancher of some authority in that little Texas town—a man who after dinner chewed a cigar and talked low cow prices with Damon's daddy. Already he was stewing about next year's election—the way the Democrats were lining up behind "that Kennedy fellow." Floyd was a heavy man. Thirty years of smoking had left him with damaged lungs. He talked in short breathy exhalations.

"Yankee boy. He'll turn his back...on us Americans," Floyd said, "if we get in a tight...with the Russians...mark my words."

He gestured with his cigar, aimed its ash at his brother-in-law as if it were a missile. "Yankee boy...he'll call on the Pope...when he can't figure out what to do." Floyd bolted upright then with a deep cough.

The Reverend Wallace Wilson watched and listened. At times he tried to temper Uncle Floyd's opinions with some injunction from one of his recent sermons, a sermon that his brother-in-law had most likely slept through. But most times Damon's daddy remained quiet, as if he had used his store of words in the Sunday night sermon and was left half-mute, resigning himself to chew vigorously on a stick of Juicy Fruit gum to ward off the temptation of one of Floyd's cigars.

Even though it was 1959, Uncle Floyd had not purchased a television set, believed it to be an expensive fad whose time would soon pass. So after a while Damon tired of Uncle Floyd's right-field theories. He wandered out to the detached garage where Farris fiddled under the hood of his '55 Chevy. Farris' three older brothers had already left home and he was always fiddling with one thing or the other. Iris Wilson theorized that Farris missed his brothers, but her husband opined that Farris needed a part-time job. "He's the baby—it's as simple as that—and Nell's spoiled him rotten."

A bare overhead bulb hung from an electric cord in the garage and the Chevy, two-tone green and white, gleamed in the harsh light.

"You want to go for a spin?" Farris asked. He didn't look at Damon when he spoke, probably not wanting to acknowledge that his social life for the evening might have to include his shy, skinny cousin.

Damon shrugged. "I guess so," he said. "I'll have to ask Daddy."

Farris looked exasperated. He pulled a half-empty packet of

Beechnut from his hip pocket and crammed a stringy wad of it in the back of his jaw. Damon waited to see if Farris would offer a chew to him, but he didn't.

"Well, get a move on then. If you want to go." Farris buttoned his jacket, a football letter jacket with crazed leather sleeves that one of his older brothers had won in high school. "It's too cold to wait around out here, though, so get the lead out."

His daddy gave a distracted, annoyed nod when Damon asked permission to go off with his older cousin, the Reverend Wilson transferring to Damon his dazed inattention, his impatience with his opinionated brother-in-law. Wallace was ready to be done with this Sunday evening fol-de-rol so that he could get on home. Floyd was now plowing new ground, moving into the federal feedgrain program where farmers got paid tax dollars not to grow grain crops. "The Reds...they're behind it," Floyd said, looking around to see if anyone was listening. He eyed Damon suspiciously and waited, clamping down on his cigar until Damon's daddy had absentmindedly nodded yes to the boy, and Damon had hurried out the door.

The main street of the town was paved in red brick, worn glassy slick from eighty years of rain and wind and traffic. Red brick buildings lined either side of the street. They were mostly two-storey, their upper levels dark, some of the windows sheathed with plywood rectangles. The drug store and the Green and White Grocery and Farmers' State Bank all glowed, the way they did every Christmas season, their edges outlined with hundreds of sparkling white lights.

The Chamber of Commerce had somewhere found—and erected at the end of the street—a giant armature of a man, a metal skeleton that soared forty feet into the air and rested on two spread-apart trunk-like legs.

The town merchants had draped this monster in a Santa Claus

suit, using scores of yards of red flannel and black leatherette. The local gin donated half a bale of raw cotton for the beard and the top notch on the cap. This massive Santa was intended to draw hordes of tourists and shoppers the sixty miles down from Dallas, but had served mostly to attract teenagers in from the suffocating plainness of their overheated farm houses. They drifted up and down the street, competing to see who could best maneuver their daddys' pickup trucks between Santa's immense black boots.

Farris cruised Main Street with his cousin Damon leaning out the car window in spite of the cold, gawking up at Santa's crotch and belly each time they made a pass through his legs. The car radio could only pick up a couple of stations at night. Farris fiddled with the knob, Fats Domino fading in and out, his voice crackling with static. Farris was alert to every car and pickup that rattled along the three blocks of brick street. He rolled his window down every few passes, pulling in close to some other bored teenagers and exchanging exaggerated stories of boys from other towns invading Haley trying to pick up the local girls, or that the "state highway boys" had set up a radar trap out on Highway 31 just west of town.

Billy Ray Davis and Royce Babcock waved Farris down. Billy Ray filled up the driver's seat of his mother's ancient Buick, and was careful—stretching his head out the window when he spit—not to spray the car's shiny finish with tobacco juice. "Spotted me a nigger," he said. "A big buck. This side of Tyner's store."

"This side, huh? He headed this way?" Farris spit, wiped the back of his hand across the leg of his jeans.

Billy Ray shrugged. "Was. This side of the store," he said. "Out on the Southtown Road. The boy should know better."

"We could tell Buddy," Royce said. He leaned forward from the passenger side of the Buick. Royce's wide-set eyes bugged a little and he blinked too often when he talked. "After dark like this, Buddy'll run him back south if he don't run him in."

Farris checked his rearview mirror. Buddy Bounds was back up Main Street, always watching. He was the town's lone constable, a barrel-chested, skinny-legged man with a withered left arm and a bobbing Adam's apple who worked nights only. He strung a single red flasher on a black cord that connected to the cigarette lighter of his '53 Pontiac, and ran the cord out the driver's window and set it askew on the top of his car. He made sure the teenagers stayed on the sober and sane side of fistfights, and that no drag racing occurred within sight of Main Street.

At six in the morning Buddy Bounds would pull away from his spot on Main Street and turn the law enforcement duties over to Sheriff Kenny Carter and his roving litter of deputies. They were responsible for the entire county, but hardly ever left Corsicana, the county seat, preferring to remain in close proximity to the amenities of that larger town with its Pitt Grill and Sunshine Donut Shop and the potential of drama out on the interstate that divided Corsicana, east and west, black and white.

"Yeah," Farris said, sarcasm heavy in his voice. "We damn sure could tell Buddy. Or we could take care of that boy ourselves."

Billy Ray grinned. "You got a four-door. We'll go with you." He peeled off just enough to get Buddy's attention, but not enough to stir the constable into action, and parked nose-in to the high curb. Farris pulled his Chevy close, let it idle, then raced the engine, looking proud, admiring the smooth power of the engine, the soft puff and blat of the twin Smittys.

Billy Ray and Royce eased out of the Buick, stood there in the street a minute gazing up at the Santa Claus. "Big fucker, ain't he," Billy Ray said.

"Belly's bigger than yours," Farris said with a laugh.

"He ain't baby Jesus, for damned sure," Billy Ray said.

"What do you mean by that?" Farris asked.

"Just what I said. He ain't baby Jesus."

"Dumb fucker," Farris said.

Royce and Billy Ray slid into the back seat. They nodded at Damon—knew who he was, for everyone in Haley knew everyone else. Damon was the preacher's boy, Farris' little cousin.

Farris wheeled the Chevy around. With a whoop he accelerated between Santa's legs and took a right down the gravel clatter of a side street. It seemed that Farris had thought this out, for he headed straight to the Methodist Church, where he circled the block once.

"Not the goddamned church, old buddy," Royce said. "We can't steal from the Methodist Church. Not with Preacher's Boy along." He shook his head.

"Hell if we can't," Billy Ray said.

"Borrow," Farris said. "Not steal. We'd never steal from a church," and the three boys hooted and laughed. Billy Ray slipped into the night and headed for a stack of two-by-fours. He managed to work a ten-foot board free, but in doing so, toppled the whole pile of lumber. It fell with a clatter and a crash. He grabbed the board and raced back to the car.

"The son-of-a-bitch is wet," he complained, for a light mist had fallen most of the afternoon.

"Tough titty," Farris said. "Duty calls."

The board stuck a couple of feet out each side of both back seat windows. "Buddy might not like the way this here looks," Royce said. "Let's get the hell out."

"You think Buddy Bounds gives a royal crap about a nigger..." Billy Ray said, "...a hard-headed nigger edging around white town? Shit, we're just doing his job. He'd appreciate the hell out of it." Billy Ray was the biggest of the boys, a guard on the Haley Hornet's football team. As a sophomore he had made second team All-District, which elevated him to local hero status.

Farris stayed to the side roads in town, past the simple cottages and the occasional two-story antebellum imitation that had been financed by high-cotton dollars and near-slave labor in the twenties. After a half-dozen blocks of loose gravel streets, the town petered out into blank fields.

Farris swung the Chevy up onto the hard surface of the Southtown road. There they eased along checking the shoulders of that road, eyeing the side lanes that led into the fields. Here and there a house sat isolated back from the road, a dim-lit cube trapped by a choppy sea of black furrows.

They passed Tyner's store. In the dim yellow lights of that tin box, they could make out Red Tyner behind the counter. And Damon suddenly could smell the store, the wood smoke from the pot-bellied stove, the rotting heads of iceberg lettuce, the raw beef and pork and chickens and the sawdust on the floor behind the meat counter. On a dismal night like this, old man Tyner would be totaling up the day's measly charges, counting the few worn and rumpled bills he had taken in, shutting the place down.

"What do you think?" Farris lifted his head back and up towards Billy Ray. "Where'd your boy disappear to?"

"Maybe he's on down a little ways," Billy Ray said. "He was north of the store not thirty minutes ago and headed towards town. Had a limp, a bad leg or something. Maybe high on some home brew. I dunno. But he had no business being there. Not this time of night."

"Shit," Royce muttered. "Can't nigger-knock a cripple. And hell, he ain't here now. He's probably headed back to nigger town. Shit, let's toss this damned two-by-four, roll up the damned windows. Get a chili dog before Maudie's closes. I'm about to freeze my ass back here."

"You can toss your two-by-four," Farris said, slowing the car, pointing up ahead. "In about two minutes. Right after we teach this boy a lesson."

Royce and Billy Ray leaned forward so they could see. Royce said "Oh, shit," under his breath, and Damon couldn't tell if his exclamation was one of anticipation or of dread.

Then, for those few dark seconds, Damon could only watch, immobile in the front seat. He wanted to cry out for Farris to stop. He had an urge to reach out for the steering wheel and swerve the car back to the left. But things happened too fast, he would later remember. Fast and strangely slow at the same time. Hauntingly slow later, when those few seconds flashed forever across his mind's eye.

There was Farris' skinny hand gripping the steering wheel of the car, his hand blue-veined in the dash lights, the hand gripping so tight that Damon thought he could see the outline of hand bones under the chalky skin.

He glanced back up. Ahead and a little to the right, at the end of the car's bright lights, a man staggered along the edge of the road heading away from town, his back to the approaching Chevy. Damon shifted to his right, ducked his head a little and without thinking aimed straight at the man's back, using as his sight a star-like gravel ding in the windshield glass. He gave a silent click with his tongue, the sort of click he used when he aimed his BB gun, the kind of click he used when he rode with his daddy and lined up highway signs and birds on a wire and men in fields riding their tractors. Not a "Bang, you're dead!" sort of click, but simply an unconscious lining up, an ordering of what was before him. More of a camera click, a way to freeze objects in the frame of his mind. Harmless.

Behind Damon, Royce rolled his window all the way down, the two-by-four dropping fast. Billy Ray pushed it out until he held the board by one end, a good five feet now sticking out of the car and into the dark night. Farris slowed and swerved onto the shoulder, the gravel spraying up and out, the headlights bouncing, and still the black man trudged on with a limp and a lurch. Damon couldn't tell if the man was drunk or lame, but thought that any moment he surely would step aside and leap across the slick-bottom of the bar ditch until the car had safely passed.

But the man never broke his limp/lurch gait, never turned his head at all. He was like a miler who refused to break his stride at the tape, to scramble at the finish, even if maintaining the discipline of his stride meant defeat.

When the board struck the man Damon cried out, some unintelligible word or words that bolted from him, beyond his willing, and his cry mixed with that crackthud and Billy Ray's yelp of sharp pain and a curse from Farris as he swung the car back onto the hard surface of the road. They rolled forward, the car slowing, then stopped.

"God almighty damn," Royce said. Then he said it again, "God almighty damn," as the car whined in reverse, and with Farris turned in his seat, they swerved back to where the man lay face down on the wet ground.

Farris stopped when the car lights illuminated the man. The wet, slick-worn soles of his heel-up boots gleamed in the night, but the rest of his body seemed to be a void, more a rumple of dark clothes than a man. Except for his head, for the base of his head had taken the blow, and was disfigured with a blood-gushing gash, and his neck was skewed at an odd angle.

Damon leaned forward against the car's dashboard, and felt for a moment that he would throw up at his feet.

"God almighty damn," Royce whispered now for the third time. "Why didn't he dodge? Hell, it was his fault. The son of a bitch never even looked back."

"Dumb-ass nigger," Billy Ray said, between short, hard gasps of breath.

"Yeah," Royce said. "You're right. It was his own damned fault."

Damon looked over at Farris, pleading for this not to really have happened. He wished for this to be a game, one set up to scare the preacher's boy. But one glance at Farris, his face white, drawn tight in the dashlight glow, and Damon knew this was no game. Still Farris forced a shaky grin. "One less nigger, boys."

Billy Ray, with his good hand, shoved the board on out the window where it fell with a clatter.

Farris screwed around in his seat, glaring at Billy Ray. "Get it," he said, and now his grin had vanished. "Get the goddamned board!"

Billy Ray only seemed able to cradle his arm and moan, so Royce hopped out and retrieved the two-by-four. He stuck it back through the open window, being careful not to touch its blood-stained end. The car got silent a minute and Damon heard Royce loose a sob, an unnatural catch of hard breath from somewhere deep. Farris raced the engine and popped the clutch, the Chevy peeling off down the slick road, the rear end whipping side to side before straightening out with its tires and gears finally in sync, racing all the way to the turn-off for the county dump.

Damon braced himself, his hand extended to the dashboard. Again, without thinking, he moved his head so that this hand lined up with the edge of the road.

Damon held his aim as steady as he could with the bounce and sway of the car, steady, the way he had learned to aim his first BB gun—he must have been eight or nine—a Red Ryder lever-action model that held scores of BBs. He had stalked sparrows that nested around the eaves of his house, imagining his hunting to be sniper patrol in the Korean War. He shot at those pesky sparrows several times, but the BBs pinged harmlessly off the gutters and the roof's metal flashing. But one day he spotted a mockingbird on a wire. Without thinking, without consciously aiming, he pulled the gun to his shoulder and fired—the gray and white feathered bird dropped. He remembered his surprise at hitting the bird, followed immediately by a rush of regret, and an almost intolerable sadness as he held the warm weight of the bird in his hand. Its eyes stared up at him with an empty gloss.

Tonight was different. Damon had not held the board, and had not driven the car. But he had not said no to Farris, had not opted to go back to the boring safety of Uncle Floyd's house when he knew that he should.

And that was no mockingbird lying still warm and very dead back up the dark road.

Chapter 2

It was almost eleven when Farris dropped Damon off at his house. The street had fallen quiet, the mist—now lessened—had turned into a vaporous fog. After Farris pulled softly away, Damon stood outside his house in the cold, pulling his windbreaker close around for comfort. He waited under the glare of a gable-mounted light that flooded the front walk's stepping stones and the side beds of barren rose bushes.

The house had been built some years earlier as a simple box, clad with gray asbestos siding that enclosed two bedrooms and a living room and a kitchen and a bath. When the local Methodists purchased the house for their parsonage (seen as a strategy for paying their resident minister an even lower salary), they closed in the back porch for another room, now Damon's bedroom. It was a long, narrow space with windows all across the back, the coldest room in the winter.

At the front door a doormat incongruously proclaimed "Bienvenidos"—the doormat a going-away gift when the

Reverend and Iris Wilson left that last church of his, a South Texas congregation that had once seemed to be the last and final slide-stop on a career gone sour, when miraculously, rescue came as an opportunity to come back home—home for Iris Wilson, at least—back to Haley, back among her people. For Haley was the place where she grew up. Wallace Wilson jumped at it, for he had to jump somewhere, the Mexican-Americans in that small South Texas community having jumped before him—away from the stodginess of the traditional Methodist Church to the invading Latter Day Saints, or out on the highway to the new metal building the Assembly of God holy rollers had thrown up. Some fell back on the Mother Church, the little Catholic parish on the hill at the edge of town.

Anywhere but to Wallace's church, a Methodist mission beachhead that had never quite caught on there. With Reverend Wilson's exit, the church had shut down, the failure being easily heaped on Wallace Wilson's not-so-strong shoulders. There was, he admitted to Iris, a sense of relief to be back with the familiar, but he hated the resignation he felt, for at forty-eight he was too young to give up. He would see. Perhaps this time in Haley would serve as a sabbatical of sorts, he told himself, but he feared in his heart that he might never—ever—get Iris to venture out again.

Damon waited, dreading to step onto that Bienvenidos doormat, for he picked up a faint glow from the front room. At first he thought it might be the Christmas tree lights, but the glow flashed and leapt from the darkness, evidence that his daddy was still up, staring at Johnny Carson or some late night movie. Maybe he wouldn't have to face his mother though, for she hardly ever stayed up late.

Damon eased the door open—it was never locked. In the half-light of the room he could make out the shiny waves of his daddy's head over the back of the recliner. The room was silent, the volume on the television all the way down, and for a moment

Damon's hopes rose. Maybe his daddy had fallen asleep, and he could slip silently across the shag rug and the slick pine floors and down the narrow hallway past all of the framed photographs—the generations of upright and honorable ancestors that now would bear witness to his guilt.

But suddenly Wallace Wilson sat straight up and in a moment had pushed himself from the chair and faced his son. Damon had never seen him move so fast, for Wallace carried a heft, a barrel chest that had fallen over the years leaving him with a more than ample girth. The Reverend Wilson had kept his beard, the beard he grew in seminary where he was older than many of the other students. The beard and the worried brow reminding Damon of some character in a movie, maybe Little John in "The Adventures of Robin Hood." A not-so-jolly, not-so-carefree version of Little John.

Now Wallace appeared disoriented, as if he had awakened from a deep sleep and was confused by where he found himself. "Son," he said. His deep voice filled the room. "Where have you been, son?"

Now Damon confronted a choice. He could tell the truth. Or he could lie. He hadn't thought about it—what story he would tell, not concretely. About when the four boys slipped into Corsicana on the south road and cut through the dilapidation of Southtown, past the cotton gin, and turning right, followed the railroad tracks until they crossed Beaton Street. There they turned left, Farris giving out an exaggerated sigh of relief when he spotted the giant cone with a curl on top lit up just ahead, and the confusion of cars nosed in at the Dairy Mart.

There had been no time for Damon to think at all, not when Billy Ray, minus his usual swagger, sidled up to the prettiest of the Corsicana girls, a girl tight-wrapped in her boyfriend's letter jacket, her boyfriend's arm around her shoulder, and spoke those words to her that Farris had instructed him to speak.

And the boy came at Billy Ray, and Billy Ray, despite his good intentions, despite Farris' instructions, didn't swing his broken hand but swung wildly with his one good arm, until the fist fight aborted into a wrestling match, both boys grappling, then hitting and rolling over the hood of the car, before tumbling to the oil-stained concrete of the parking lot.

He had no time to think while Royce and Farris pulled the thrashing boys apart and hustled a moaning Billy Ray into the back seat where he rocked and spluttered and cursed and held his injured wrist all the way to the Navarro County Hospital emergency room.

And on the way back to Haley, Damon was too taken over by Farris' words, the words of what to say and what not to say and what to do and how to act, words that Damon felt imprinted in his brain—like a P.O.W. from the Korean War in the hands of the Chinese Reds—so intent was he on the words that came so easily, so convincingly, from Farris' mouth. But they were not Damon's words.

Damon had been the last of the three boys that Farris dropped off, the other two moving from Chevy to Buick right there on Main Street under the watchful, disapproving eye of Constable Buddy Bounds. If there had been some alternative to going home, Damon would have jumped at it. Running away slipped in and then out as a possibility—the thought not absolutely new, but never before seriously entertained. But Haley had no bus station, and now the passenger trains raced through Corsicana without slowing on their irregular Dallas-to-Houston runs, and hitchhiking—waiting out on the highway in that freezing mist for God only knows what late-night character to come along—sent an involuntary shiver through him.

Farris had eased down the side streets of town, the thin gravel veneer of the rain-soft streets giving way under the weight of the car, leaving smooth ruts trailing behind. There were no curbs, the streets blending smoothly into winter-gray Bermuda grass lawns that crept and dipped into drainage ditches and spread stringy runners onto the edge of the road.

And now, as Damon stood before his father, an answer flashed into his twelve-year-old brain, a way to handle the events of the night. What he told would be the truth, for he was his daddy's son, and the truth and the importance of the truth had swirled around him from his infancy until now.

His daddy's question: "Where have you been?"

"Corsicana," Damon said quietly, deliberately, easily, now without fear, now that he had resolved to tell the truth. "Farris wanted to go over to Corsicana. He picked up a couple of his friends and we all went over to Corsicana. We hung out around the Dairy Mart. For a while." His voice was even, matter of fact, and he heard his words come out as if they were detached from him, had originated in some other unknown person who had temporarily taken over his body. Like "The Thing from Another World," he thought, and he felt the faint beginnings of a smile on his lips. But the detachment of the words couldn't smother the churning of his stomach. Damon's mother showed up then, just appeared suddenly in the doorway to the hall, her housecoat loose around her, a couple of pin curls bobby-pinned above her ears. Or maybe she had been there all along, listening. "He's too young for that," she said, aiming her words at her husband, but staring all the while at Damon.

Damon chose his words carefully. "Daddy said I could go."

"Not to Corsicana." Wallace started to pace, a pacing that seemed cramped and hopeless in the small room. Then he stopped. "Not out of town. Now you know that, son."

Damon shrugged. The truth was not easy, he knew, and he had not explored its latitudes this way before.

"You need to pay more attention, Wallace." His mother's words were cold as the night air. "Listen to him when he talks to you. You're always off someplace else when you should be listening." She gave a little "off someplace else" sign, a little twirl of her hand, her finger pointed upwards towards the ceiling.

Another tactic, Damon realized. A tactic to use while still holding steadfast to particular strands of truth. Turn the argument around. If you are accused, then accuse back. Or better yet, have someone else do it for you.

Wallace held up his hand as if he were silencing his congregation. "What friends went along? Who are Farris' friends anyway?"

Damon said their names—Billy Ray Davis and Royce Babcock. The truth told once more. This was easier than he had figured.

"Oh," his mother said, and waited, silently, not fishing for words—for she had the words, was never without words. But for a moment she held them back, just shook her head. Then she spoke, still aiming the words at her husband. "Those two are nothing but trouble, Daddy. That Davis boy is a bully, and the Babcocks are trash."

"I know who they are, Mother." Wallace had had enough, had grown impatient with his reticent son, with the quick, sharp judgments—the unfair judgments, he thought—of his wife. "Go on to bed now, son. It's late. But I don't want this happening again. Do you understand?"

Damon understood. This night would never happen again. But it had happened. He felt uneasy with the way he had played with the truth. He felt as if something still hung in his gut, something that he needed to throw up on the shine of the pine floor he stood on. He felt himself silently pleading for his daddy to probe further, to pull the truth from him.

Damon left the room, turned sideways to pass by his mother. He turned away from her, but still caught the rose petal scent of face cream or shampoo as he passed, and the look of disapproval that he knew she held on him until he was in his room. Then she could turn her disapproval back to her husband—a man who, despite his late-blooming heft, she could see right through, past the resonant timbre of his voice, the voice that coated and smoothed and polished the most ordinary of words until they gleamed. A man who held himself with a certain bearing, a prideful bearing, more appropriate for an Anglican priest than for a small-town Methodist preacher. She saw through, had lived through, the veneer of his pious and devout Sunday sermons. She knew him—knew his ordinariness, his private fustiness, his crankiness, his transparent imposturing. Iris knew his deceit and his betrayal. Goodwill towards men was a nice ideal, but goodwill between Iris and Wallace would be a long time coming.

"How can a man be the moral center of his family?" Wallace later wrote in his journal after Iris had retreated to their bedroom, after "The Tonight Show" had been supplanted with a "Have Gun, Will Travel" rerun. "How, when he knows in his heart that he has lost his way, lost the respect of his wife (for good enough reasons), and lost respect for himself?" He hated his words, that pious tone, but he couldn't help himself. Then in an angry hand, the letters forced and wide, he wrote. "Why can't I simply be who I am?"

Wallace folded the journal closed, and thought of Damon. He wondered how long it would be before his son discovered that he was only a cracked shell of a man. He hugged the journal to his chest, the journal that knew his secret ruminations and even his doubts, the scribblings and random insights that fed his Sunday sermons. He moved to the kitchen and lifted an almost empty carton of ice cream from the freezer. He stood at the kitchen counter and—staring out into the fog that had fallen over the town—he spooned that sweet, smooth comfort straight from the box.

Chapter 3

THE TELEPHONE RANG EARLY. Damon heard its shrill insistence from where he lay awake in his bed. It rang in his daddy's study down the hall from Damon's room, and in the kitchen, at the opposite end of the house, where his mother answered it. The dread of the coming day had kept Damon in bed, but not asleep, and now, suddenly, he was super-alert. He pulled himself to his elbows, straining to hear. He hoped it was Aunt Nell with some gossip for his mother, or maybe wanting her to run over to Corsicana for last minute Christmas shopping at the downtown Dreyfuss Brothers department store. But his mother's voice bit the air hard and short and to the point. "Wallace," she yelled, "it's Boyd Douglas."

The Reverend Boyd Douglas ministered to the town's Baptists, took his position overseeing the biggest flock in Haley quite seriously. He was a young man, a man barely in his thirties, if that—a slight, energetic man with a plump blonde wife and two plump, always overdressed toddlers. Boyd Douglas was blessed, as some saw it—Wallace not among them—with an overflowing optimism. His favorite, overworn expression was, "If life gives you lemons, make lemonade."

Wallace saw Boyd, with his boundless enthusiasm, being out of place in this dying town, his annoying vigor more suited to directing the youth ministry in some robust Dallas church. These unshakable optimist types grated on Wallace, made him want to probe beneath their sunny dispositions and expose what breed of beast really prowled their dark souls.

Then from the study Damon heard his daddy's voice—his preacher telephone voice—cordial, concerned and caring, not betraying the resentment he felt for this cheerful young man who counted as his flock twice as many congregants as the Methodists.

Damon eased from his bed. In his pajamas he slipped down the hall towards his daddy's voice. December 24th, he thought, the day before Christmas. He wished school were not out so that he could disappear into the anonymity of a crowded, overheated classroom and not be trapped here at home.

Damon hated his daddy's study, for it was not a real study at all, but the single-car garage that had been built attached to one end of the house, and now was closed in, its wide, overhead door replaced with double, sliding glass panels that opened to the front of the house and onto the gravel driveway.

This was the room where Granny Wyrick withered away in a rented roll-up-and-down hospital bed, where Iris brought her mother soft-cooked meals three times a day, and snipped elm twigs from the backyard tree and stripped them of their bark—slick, yellow-green twigs for her mama to clean her teeth, for Granny Wyrick didn't believe in regular toothbrushes and toothpaste.

And what good came from it? Damon wondered. All of those overcooked meals, all of that bathing and turning and waking in the middle of the night, and Granny Wyrick dying there in that room after fourteen months of suffering, dead and buried now not quite a year. The room, converted to Wallace's study, still held the odor of Granny Wyrick's death.

No one else in the family seemed to notice, for Iris Pine-Sol scrubbed the floors and Wallace, with the help of a church deacon, had tacked up thin brown imitation wood-grained paneling. With obvious relief Wallace slid his file cabinet and table-for-a-desk and his curved-back, roll-around chair into the study from the bedroom that he and Iris shared.

Maybe the not-noticing was how grown-ups handled their misery. For what else had this been—the coming back to Haley—but a refusal to acknowledge their misery, some undefined price that his daddy and his mother had to pay?

Iris had seven siblings—two sisters and five brothers—most of them living within sixty miles of their old home town, but somehow not one of them could take in their mother, knowing that in the end Iris, the caretaker, would find a way.

Why hadn't they stayed in Fort Worth, Damon wondered, where his daddy had a big church and he could walk to a park that had basketball goals and a concrete court, and a swimming pool with a high diving board for the too-short summers? A city where Wallace walked briskly on the quiet streets every morning, and where Iris indulged herself by strolling, window-shopping her way through the new Neiman Marcus store out west of town.

There they had laughed, Wallace with his booming laughter filling that two-story brick parsonage, and Iris, her laughter a smothered giggle and faintly girlish, a laugh that seemed out of place, not enough of a laugh for such a strong woman. Until this moment Damon had not missed the laughter, for it was conspicuous only in its absence.

But suddenly the laughter had stopped, and a grimness without relief followed them south out of Fort Worth, far south, miles south of San Antonio to that little, mostly Mexican town where none of them fit in. And two years later it was back to Haley, hurriedly packing their worn-out belongings as if they were refugees catching the last train out—away from there with a mixture of relief and reluctance, Wallace grasping desperately for a place where he could stop his slide, leaping to whatever might keep him from sinking completely.

Now Damon stood as close to the study as he dared, afraid that his daddy would sense his presence, afraid, also, that he would catch a whiff of that foul and rotten smell, the smell of death, that repulsed him whenever he approached that room.

"No." Wallace said, drawing out the word. "Noooo"—the "No" more a groan of disbelief, than a simple word. Damon heard the squeak of his chair, the slide of his father's feet as he jerked upright in the chair. "Oh, no," he said. "I can't believe it. But yes, it's all right. Come on by. Yes, we have to, I'm afraid. I'll be ready." He hung up the phone. "Lord help us all," he muttered.

Damon slipped back to his room just ahead of his daddy who hurried past the bedroom door on his way to the kitchen, looking neither to the right or left. Damon followed behind, trying not to appear anxious. He slumped down on the living room sofa. He picked at some loose threads that Cowtown, a cat they still had from their Fort Worth days, had snagged, and listened.

"He was James Henry Brown's brother," Wallace told Iris. "Homer Crawford found him this morning. Homer was on his way to the dump, just at daylight. He thought it was a sack of rags by the side of the road at first."

"That's the law enforcement's business," Iris said. "That's for Sheriff Carter to handle. I don't see why in the world Boyd Douglas would call you. He's just a busybody as far as I can see."

"Just listen," Wallace said impatiently. "I don't know all of the details yet, but Boyd says the Sheriff has been to the site, and called it a killing. And Sheriff Carter called Boyd. Said they might need his help—and mine—to keep things calm. That's all I know. When Boyd gets here, he'll fill me in on the rest."

"The Sheriff called Boyd. He didn't call you. This is none of your business," Iris said. "Not that I don't feel sorry for Reverend Brown. Losing a brother that way would be hard, and James Henry is a good man, but there's always something bad happening down there with the nigras. And you'd do well to listen to me, Wallace Wilson. What happens down there in Southtown is none of your business, and I hope you have the good sense to stay out of it."

"I'm already in it," Wallace said. He checked the coffee maker, tossed the soggy filter in the trash under the sink. "We all are. The NAACP and the *Dallas News* reporters, maybe the FBI—they're all on their way, I'm sure. This will be all over the papers, maybe even on the national news tonight."

Wallace tried to fight off the excitement rising in his chest. For all the wrong reasons he saw this as a way to start the climb back. Wallace would be spotlighted as the voice of reason, a moderate leader in a red-neck, racist town. "It's tragic, I know, but maybe, finally, it will expose the way the Negroes are treated around here."

"Most of it they've brought on themselves," Iris said. She hesitated a moment, knew she was headed in a direction she didn't like, about to make assertions that she didn't really believe, and knew she would proclaim them anyway, right out loud and straight-faced. Not because she believed them, but because it was a way to stand up to Wallace.

She did that now and then, took unreasonable and arbitrary positions just to find some way to strike out at him. She always felt badly afterwards, but something took her over, it seemed, either anger or spite or just flat being hurt. Iris had no more control over the "why" than she had over what she might say. The words had a blast, a force that she couldn't shut down until she knew she had wounded her husband.

"They want too much, too fast," she continued while Wallace paced the room. "Before you know it they'll be mixing in the schools. And that's all right. I have nothing against the nigras. Some of them are good, honest folks. I was brought up here, though, and I understand them. And I know most of them won't change. They're not ready for all of this."

Iris turned now to look straight at Wallace. "It's impossible for some people to change overnight, no matter how well-intentioned they are." She paused a moment, just enough to let Wallace know that those last words were meant for him.

"And folks around here don't appreciate the way changes are shoved down their throats. Your problem, Wallace, is that you hung around the liberals in seminary too long. You're a city boy who has wandered off into a mesquite thicket. You just don't understand country ways."

Wallace shook his head. "It's almost 1960," he said. "Can you hear yourself? Do you really understand what you're saying?"

"Can you see yourself?" she shot back. "Who you really are?"

"That's not fair," Wallace murmured, but Iris ignored him. Maybe there was some truth in what Iris said, he thought, for he had grown up in Houston. But in those years there were no visible problems with the Negroes, mostly because they were invisible, and made no demands.

And Iris? He had never thought of her as racist. She certainly showed no evidence of it when he struggled through seminary, and in Fort Worth she was an exemplary pastor's wife in most ways, generous with her time, and putting her strong soprano voice to good use in the choir.

But back here in Haley around her people, she seemed to have reverted to someone who Wallace had never known. He took some of the blame. Maybe Iris needed comfort or needed support. Perhaps with Wallace she had become disillusioned with the church, with the imperfections that even Methodist ministers—especially one of them—had.

"Anyway," Iris went on, "You'd be well off to watch what you say. Especially what you do." Iris caught her husband's eye, froze him for just an instant. "This time everyone will be watching."

"I know, I know," he said with a wave of the hand. "But this is different." That incident in Fort Worth flashed through his mind, a simple misreading of intentions it had been, an ambiguity that an unstable woman of his congregation had misinterpreted. Harmless in and of itself, but destructive given the parties involved.

Wallace's voice dropped low, so low and desperate that Damon could barely hear him from the living room. "Won't you ever let go of the past? Can't you finally do that for me?"

Iris pulled her hands from the soapy water, held a glass, dripping in her hand. She wiped the rim with a dishcloth, and pointed it at him, as if she were taking aim. "When you have been hurt as much as you hurt me, I will," she said, and slipped the glass back down into the sudsy sink. "Only then will I let it go."

The doorbell rang. "It's Boyd," Wallace said and hurried through the living room. When he saw Damon there, sunk down on the sofa, he slowed and pulled at his dark beard as if he could somehow pull the right words from his mouth. Then—his face drawn and sad—he hurried to the front door.

Chapter 4

WALLACE DROVE. He wanted whatever control he could manage and didn't want Boyd Douglas, the fair-haired boy who rode next to him, getting the upper hand. Boyd wore shiny blue slacks and a maroon blazer. His tie had little figures stitched on it that at first glance Wallace thought were hula dancers, but to his relief turned out to be palm trees. All the way from Wallace's house into town, Boyd went on about opportunity, the way that even in the most tragic circumstances something could be learned. "Good can come out of evil," he said cheerfully , "if you trust in the Lord."

Wallace nodded, relieved that Boyd hadn't brought in the making lemonade out of lemons analogy. Once through town and past the giant Santa Claus, they hit the hard-topped road that led south, Wallace driving his Dodge sedan slowly, trying to hide his eagerness for what lay ahead.

The events of the night before were tragic. Wallace genuinely regretted the incident and its repercussions. But the bitter-sweet fruit of tragedy is drama, and Wallace now craved that drama, some emotional charge to lift him above himself. He now was ready to embrace change—almost any change—even tragic change. Anything to break the monotony. They passed by the plowed-under cotton fields, empty stretches of black-rowed ground. Some of the land had succumbed to years of farming, and now, cottoned-out, was bound by sagging four-wire fences that held skinny cows on the bare-earth pastures. A few houses sat back from the road at the ends of narrow, muddy lanes, but most of them had been relegated to make-do hay barns, and safe nesting places for varmints and owls.

Soon, in the road ahead, Wallace spotted the pulsing tempo of flashing lights against the gray sky, and a jumble of cars. As they got closer a highway patrolman with his western hat pulled down tight waved them onto the left side of the road, using a palms-down gesture to slow their speed.

A couple of sheriff's cars blocked off the right shoulder of the road, next to a green Ford sedan with blackwall tires and a tiny antenna. Undercover, Wallace figured, maybe the FBI already down from their Dallas office. Among the other half dozen cars he spotted one with *Corsicana Daily News* in script across its door.

Off to one side several black men huddled, intent, their heads together. Wallace saw the Reverend James Henry Brown in the center. He was oversized, in height and in girth—he always seemed about to burst out of his dark suit. He stood above the others who gathered around him, men in overalls and khakis and faded jackets.

Wallace stopped for the patrolman. Boyd rolled his window down. Wallace leaned to his right to speak, but Boyd beat him to it, too quickly, too enthusiastically explaining who he and Wallace were, how they might be needed "in this time of sorrow and tragedy."

The patrolman leaned down, peered over at Wallace, eyeing his beard. "You from around here?" he asked.

"Absolutely," Wallace said. "From Haley. Sheriff Carter knows me."

Boyd glanced at Wallace, a quick look of disapproval on his face. The beard, Wallace figured. Well, let them disapprove. He would be out of Haley before long, back in some civilized city where he fit in, where he could better use his talents.

The patrolman gave Wallace a skeptical look. The timing of their arrival on the scene evidently was bad, the patrolman already annoyed, Wallace surmised, by the crowd that had gathered so quickly there. "Okay," he finally said. "But stay back, away from the crime scene. You can pull off and park down there. Not too close to that bar ditch or it'll take a wrecker to pull you out."

"A lynching without a rope," the Reverend James Henry Brown said, when Wallace and Boyd joined the group of black men. He turned to them without a greeting of any sort. "And my own brother, lame in one leg from birth and unable to flee from harm's way. Struck down from behind and killed."

The handful of black men murmured in agreement. They were waiting, it seemed, for Reverend Brown to lead them in their anger.

"This is not the frontier, not the West," he said, "where a man might be murdered for revenge or for his possessions. No, my brothers, this place is as dark as the heart of the Deep South, where a man is murdered because of the color of his skin." The gathering of men murmured low, a chorus of "Amen, brother" rising from the crowd, encouraging Reverend Brown to continue.

"This might as well be Selma or Birmingham. I prayed to the Lord that we might be spared this evil. But the Lord has spoken. We must bear the cross a little longer."

He stopped then and nodded at Wallace and Boyd who stood listening a respectable distance away.

Wallace heard the Reverend Brown's words, but his eyes were back at the gathering of uniformed lawmen, taking in what must be the scene of the killing. When Boyd stepped towards the group of black men and began a little speech that sounded wooden and rehearsed, Wallace caught Reverend Brown's eye—lifting his hand in an acknowledgment of sorts—and moved away from Boyd, making his way across the mud-streaked road.

Sheriff Carter nodded when he approached, extended his hand to Wallace. The two men had worked together before, the sheriff openly appreciative of the way Wallace had stepped forward last summer to ease the tensions in the little black community not three miles south of here. Sheriff Carter stomped his lizard boots on the asphalt in an attempt to shake loose built-up globs of clay. He chewed on the stub of an unlit cigar, moving it from one corner of his mouth to the other with an ease that fascinated Wallace. Every once in a while he worked a strand of tobacco to the end of his tongue and without losing his grip on the cigar, adroitly spit it to one side.

Now Sheriff Carter shook his head, worked the cigar until he had it just right. "There seems to be no sense to this one," he said. "And I'm not jumping to any conclusions. White folks may not be involved at all, so the Reverend might as well settle down." He nodded across the road, towards Reverend Brown. "In spite of what he might want to think."

"Any ideas? Any suspects?" Wallace asked.

"The boys are checking tire tracks—we'll make some impressions. There's a set of footprints, some sneaker prints, but they're pretty dim after the drizzle last night."

"How did he die?" Wallace asked. He glanced up the road where a couple of bored highway patrolmen stood with a deputy sheriff. They were nodding, giving one-word responses to the reporter from the Corsicana paper.

Wallace checked the pavement and the graveled shoulder of the road, but couldn't see any blood. Just a churned-up place where Willie Lee Brown must have fallen, the place more disturbed in all likelihood by the man who found him and by the ambulance attendants that carried him away than by the black man's fall.

"We did find a board, a two-by-four, partially burned and still smoking down at the county dump, but it was pretty well charred. We're checking the footprints best we can.

"This boy may not have felt a thing. He had a pint of Four Roses in his jacket pocket. About empty. The autopsy and some lab work may help with that, but for sure he got slammed in the back of the head with something. That two-by-four fits the bill about right. And he was most likely pretty well potted. EMS boys said they could smell it pretty strong."

A car pulled up then and a couple of fellows eased out into the morning air. They both were young, not more than thirty, and had a look that went past confidence and over into cockiness.

"Shit," Sheriff Carter muttered. And then quickly said, "Sorry, Reverend. But it's the federal boys. I figured they'd show up for this."

"What can I do?" Wallace asked. "To help."

"Well," the sheriff said, his voice low. "If you can keep the Reverend and his boys off my tail for a while, I'd sure be obliged." He jabbed Wallace's arm with his finger, making sure that he had his attention. "I have a feeling— remote as this road is—that we're looking for somebody local. Of course, it might be the Klan; I've got a handful of possibilities that come to mind. We'll check them out. We'll sweep a pretty wide area, but my gut tells me that this is isolated, that in all likelihood whoever is responsible for this hangs out in your neck of the woods. Hell, you never really know your neighbors. Just keep your eyes and ears open." Wallace left then, even though he was curious how Sheriff Carter would manage to stay in control of things with the FBI on the scene. But the sheriff was right—Wallace's role was that of peacemaker. Right now he could see that Boyd might need some help dealing with James Henry Brown, for another pickup and an Oldsmobile with fins had pulled up in the last few minutes and now Boyd was surrounded by a dozen or more hostile black men and a couple of angry women.

"Time?" Reverend Brown said, mocking Boyd who had asked for their patience with the investigation, asked them to give Sheriff Carter a little time. "Time?" he said again, and through his anger let out a low laugh. He shook his head, gazing slowly at those around him, gathering encouragement from their nods and their murmuring. "Why, Brother Wilson," he turned to Wallace straight on, "us black folks have given you almost a hundred years of patience." The crowd of men stirred. The Reverend Brown held up his hand.

"'The meek shall inherit the earth,' our good Lord has told us, but I'm losing interest in the earth, the earth right here in this county, in this state of Texas, in this America. And I'm not interested in being meek no more." A series of "Amens" traveled through the circle that surrounded him, accompanied by nodding heads and impatient shuffling of feet.

"But the High Sheriff and his boys can have some time. Yes, us black folks will go along once more. But only until my brother is in the ground. We will mourn his passing, swallow our anger, and with love in our hearts turn the soul of my brother," and he swept his hand around once more, taking in the now silent group before him, "turn the soul of our brother in Christ over to our Heavenly Father." He slumped a little then, his shoulders visibly sagged, and he lowered his voice. But his eyes flashed dark. "In two days we will put his soul to rest, place his battered body in this dark earth."

Reverend Brown paused a moment, and Wallace said, "Wednesday" softly to himself. "The day after Christmas."

"But after that," the Reverend Brown continued, now raising his voice, directing his gaze towards Sheriff Carter, and then intently back to the two white preachers before him, "after the Lord has received the soul of my brother, I make you no promises. None whatsoever."

Chapter 5

DAMON SLIPPED OUT OF THE HOUSE, wheeling his bike from under an overhang next to the storage shed. In a moment he was pedaling, standing and pumping hard, down the gravel street.

He slowed when he rounded the first corner and slid the bike to a stop. He stood, straddling the bike, in front of Jimmy Shaver's house, hoping that his buddy would see him waiting. For Damon hated going to the door, afraid of Jimmy's father who seemed to be a nice enough man when he was directing the high school marching band, but turned into a bear if he had been in Dallas late the night before.

Jimmy's daddy led two lives—Damon knew it, and most folks in town knew it. Raymond Shaver could play the saxophone and the clarinet and the trombone all proficiently enough to sit in with a trio that worked some of the Dallas clubs on weekend nights. During the week he taught freshman math and brought some degree of order and musicality to the school's marching band.

Jimmy laughed when he told Damon how his daddy would

sneak a case of beer and a bottle of whiskey home from Dallas late at night, and the next weekend carry the empties in a garbage bag back to Dallas. In Haley he was afraid to put the beer cans in his trash, knowing that word of his drinking might get out. For Haley was dry—the entire county was dry, in fact—and drinking by a school teacher would not be tolerated by the school board or by any of the town's three churches.

Damon and Jimmy had hit it off, for reasons they couldn't understand—one bearing the burden of "preacher's boy," and the other holding tight to the secret life his daddy lived.

Damon circled around on the street in front of the house and was about to ride off when the front door slammed and Jimmy raced for his bike. "Bastard," Jimmy said.

"You want a preacher for a daddy instead?" Damon asked. Jimmy grinned and shook his head. They headed towards town, slowed down when they hit Main Street's slick bricks, then cruised around the giant Santa's legs, made circle eights, guiding the bikes with no hands. For a few minutes they sat on one of Santa's boots. Now and then a car eased by—little kids stuck their heads out the windows, staring open-mouthed towards the giant that towered over them.

"What a fake," Jimmy said, staring up into Santa's overhanging belly. In the daylight the armature showed through the fabric and the boys could see the cotton seeds still in his beard.

"Yeah," Damon said, but he was lost in the night before, the way Farris had raced his Chevy between those trunk-like legs before taking off into the darkness. If the Santa hadn't been here, Damon thought, then Farris wouldn't have asked me to come along.

"We rode through here last night," Damon said. "Me and Farris, in his Chevy."

"Farris? Your smart aleck cousin?" Jimmy asked.

"Yeah," Damon said. He picked at a grass burr stuck to the tire of his bike. Hoped he wouldn't have a flat. "We rode around a lot. Went to the Dairy Mart in Corsicana. Billy Ray and Royce went with us."

"Billy Ray? That big asshole."

"He got in a fight. Broke his hand."

"Wow," Jimmy said. "Did your mom and dad know you went."

"Shoot no. Not 'til I got back. Then I caught the devil. It was after eleven. Man, were they mad." Damon waited, wanting Jimmy to ask him more. They were best friends. Jimmy would never tell on him no matter what.

Suddenly a car swerved in close to where the boys sat. It was Farris, his bony elbow pointing out the window. Billy Ray sat up front. Damon could see his fingers, pudgy and pink, sticking out the end of a cast that went halfway to his elbow. Royce was slumped down in the back seat.

Farris motioned for Damon to come over. He gave Jimmy a smirky grin. Damon felt himself tense up. He didn't want to talk to Farris, but he shuffled the few steps to his cousin's car.

"Let's take a little ride," Farris said.

Royce leaned over, popped open the back door. Damon glanced back at Jimmy, his hand on the door handle.

"We'll be right back," Farris said, and Jimmy gave a shrug, as if it didn't matter.

Damon eased into the backseat. He nodded at Royce, but Royce kept his bug eyes fixed on the back of Billy Ray's orange burr head. Billy Ray turned, glared at Damon, his big head like a jack o'lantern on his thick neck.

"I reckon old Jimmy there is your good buddy," Farris said as he pulled away from the Santa Claus.

Damon nodded. Royce had a Corsicana paper on the seat between them. The front page headlined rising alfalfa hay prices, had a drawing underneath of a cow munching on dollar bills. Tomorrow's paper would tell a different story.

"You make it in all right? Last night?" Farris asked. "Were your folks still up?"

Damon nodded.

"Shit," Farris moved his head to spit and Damon leaned to one side. "I was afraid of that. But it was okay? You kept things—the important things—to yourself."

"Told Daddy the truth," Damon said, and Farris flushed. "I mean, I answered his questions. Told him about going to Corsicana, about Billy Ray's fight."

"That's all?"

"That's all he asked. I'm not gonna lie. Not to my daddy."

"Well, you might have to lie," Farris said, his words spitting out in a harsh whisper. "Now Royce here, he woke up with some second thoughts, figured that since we didn't intend to—you know—we didn't mean to do more than scare that nigger, that we should come forward with our story. Tell it all, take our lumps."

Farris caught Damon's eyes in the rearview mirror. "Now that would be a dumbass thing to do. And now Royce understands that." He half turned in his seat. "Don't you Royce? Tell the preacher's boy that you understand that now."

"Yeah," Royce said, ducking his head, staring at his own hands, the way his fingers were entwined.

"Tell him then, goddamn it," Farris said.

"It'd be dumb," Royce said.

"To what?" Farris said. "It'd be dumb to what?"

"To tell," Royce said. "But it was an accident," he blurted out. "I wasn't even holding the board. You know that. Not with my hands. I just leaned against it to protect myself."

"Goddamn it, Royce," Farris said. "How many times do I have

to hear that? And how many times do I have to tell you that in the eyes of the law it don't matter. If you held the board or held onto your tiny bone of a prick. It don't matter. You're guilty. The same way the preacher's boy is, too."

Farris took a deep breath then. He made a U-turn before he got to the highway. "So, what advice do you have for my little cousin?"

"It'd be a dumbass thing to tell," Royce said. He still hadn't looked up, hadn't seen the two shiny cars that sped through town, the black men in their suits and ties that filled those two cars.

"A new development," Farris said. He reached for a tin can on the dash, held it to his thin bottom lip and spit a stream of tobacco juice. Then his eyes once more locked onto Damon in the mirror. "Bad news and good news, as they say. Bad news is that the boy we cold-cocked is Preacher James Henry Brown's oldest brother. So there'll be some holy hell raised by that big-talking nigger preacher.

"But word has it that Mr. Willie Lee Brown had a pint of hooch in his coat pocket when he met his unfortunate fate. Old Man Crawford who found him is telling that around town. A bottle with no more than a couple of good swigs left in the bottom. That's why he didn't have the sense to move out of the way, the sense that even a bitch dog in heat would have had.

"And how did Mr. Willie Lee Brown get that pint of hooch on a Sunday night? Why, from Red Tyner, that's how, that old fox bootlegging the booze all this time. And we thought he was a nigger lover for sure. Loved that liquor money. That's what."

Farris pulled up next to the Santa Claus. Jimmy was no longer there. Damon's bike was still propped against Santa's boot. Farris turned in his seat. "So we just need to be patient. Billy Ray's patient." Billy Ray nodded his big head, his eyes hardly more than slits. "And if you two will just cool your burners, this whole thing will shift. Shift to where it belongs, to Red Tyner and his bootlegging and to the niggers always gettin' liquored up and stumbling back to Southtown. And who gives a shit about a dead nigger, anyway? So keep this to yourself, and it will work its way out. You hear?"

Damon nodded.

"Can't hear you," Farris said.

"I'll keep it to myself," Damon said. "But I still won't lie."

"Shit." Farris said. He struck the steering wheel hard. He looked over at Billy Ray, slipped the Chevy back in first gear. "The truth or lies," Farris said, his words even now, smooth. "You know it don't matter. They're just a bunch of words, anyway."

He revved his engine, and the soft blat of the mufflers spilled out behind him. A car moved down Main Street towards them, then hurried on by. A couple of strangers, men in Stetson hats with no-nonsense looks on their faces sat up ramrod-straight in the front seat.

"Shit," Farris said. "Now there's Texas Rangers in town. Damned cops are everywhere." He turned back to Damon. "Before you even think about telling anything important to your preacher-man daddy, or to your mama, or to your buddy Jimmy, you better think twice." Then his words came out with a soft spray of spittle. "Me and Billy Ray'll hang your nasty ass from that Santa Claus belt and drop you on your preacher-boy's head. You understand me?" Damon pushed open the door and stepped out. He slammed the door, harder than he meant to. He could feel himself flush and his blood seemed to drain away. The Chevy eased on down the street and Damon stood there watching until—with a spin of its tires—it disappeared down a side street.

Jimmy wheeled up beside him. "What a bastard," he said. "What'd he want, anyway?"

"Nothin'," Damon said. Then he remembered his vow to tell

the truth. "He didn't want me to do nothin'." He nodded his head then as if to affirm that truth to himself.

⁂

AT NOON DAMON AND JIMMY MEANDERED through town the long way. Out on the highway they circled Maudie's Cafe to take in the aroma of frying chicken and fried potatoes and pounded and pulverized and chicken-fried round steak. Damon wished he had some nickels so they could play the pin ball machine by the front door.

But Damon was both broke and starved so the boys crossed the highway, and raced across the gravel streets until Jimmy, with a wave, turned off and wheeled towards his house.

The carport at home was empty. Damon hoped that his daddy had come back and he and Iris had taken off for some last minute shopping. He hoped they would get him a tennis racket for Christmas, but he knew that wouldn't happen in Haley. Maybe they've both driven over to Corsicana, he thought, Christmas shopping.

But Iris was in the kitchen, in the middle of mixing a bowl of cream cheese and canned fruit cocktail and mayonnaise that looked awful. Her little plastic radio sat back on the cabinet and she was singing along to Perry Como. She half-sang, half-hummed, "Catch a Falling Star," going back and forth from the melody to alto harmony. She looked up, startled when Damon came in.

"My goodness, son," she said. "I kept expecting your daddy to drive up, and here you slip in on me."

Damon shrugged. "I got hungry," he said. "What's that?" he asked, with a frown.

"I guess I'm just jumpy. With what happened last night, and everything." With a wooden spoon Iris scooped the fruit salad into a couple of empty ice trays. "You'll like it," she said. "You like everything that's in it, so you've got to like it. But it's not for today, it's for tomorrow, for Christmas dessert. I wanted to do something special."

"Are the pies for Christmas, too?" he asked, eyeing two pecan pies cooling on the stove-top.

Iris shook her head. "You can have anything but the pies. Just help yourself. There's some red beans on the stove and some corn bread sticks in the oven staying warm. Mellorine's in the freezer for dessert—unless your daddy finished it off last night." She gave out a sigh.

Damon picked up the irritation in her voice, but it confused him. She didn't act irritated, busy working on the holiday meals as if Santa Claus, or Jesus Christ himself, would be sitting down to Christmas dinner with them.

Iris slid the trays of the fruit concoction into the boxy freezer inside the refrigerator. "No Mellorine." She turned then, wiping her hands on a dishcloth. "Farris stopped by. He honked out front two or three times. I wasn't about to go out, not even to the porch. So he finally came to the door. I let him have it then, told him that honking out front was lazy and rude and he could wait out front from now on if he expected me to jump when he honked."

"I saw him in town," Damon said. "Me and Jimmy were riding around the Santa Claus down there, and he stopped by."

"Jimmy and I," Iris said.

Damon nodded. "Jimmy and I."

"What in the world did Farris want?" Iris asked. "He asked if you were around, where you had gone. Odd. He acted odd. But Farris always acts odd, as far as I'm concerned."

Damon busied himself in the refrigerator, pulling out a jar of peanut butter, a quart jug of milk, a can of chocolate syrup.

"The beans are perfectly good," Iris said, "and good for you, besides."

"Yes, ma'am," Damon said. But he pulled a loaf of white bread from the bread box on the cabinet, and smeared a slice with a thick layer of peanut butter. Iris sighed and turned back to the sink, and Damon quickly licked the knife.

"You never answered me," Iris said, turning back to face him. "What is Farris doing coming around here, looking for you? He's too old, and besides he should have his own friends."

A whole variety of answers skimmed through his brain, but none of them seemed plausible. He thought about the promise he had made to himself not to lie. And he was still trying to sort out Farris' words, the way his older cousin had so confidently claimed that truth and lies were only words and didn't matter anyway.

Iris rinsed the mixing bowl in the sink. Damon waited for her to turn the water off. He knew she would turn to face him then and would press for an answer he couldn't give.

Just as she turned towards him, drying the bowl with a dish-cloth, Damon dropped the slice of bread, peanut butter side down. It hit the floor with a heavy plop. "Shit," Damon said.

"Damon!" Iris yelled. He knelt to clean the mess up off the floor, but his mother yelled again. "To your room, young man! What in heaven's name has gotten into you? That kind of language in our house. I won't allow it. Go on, right now, and stay there until your father comes home." She reached down with a wet dish rag and scooped most of the mess off the floor.

"I'm sorry," he said. "Mama, I'm really sorry." Damon moved slowly towards his room and felt tears well up hot in his eyes.

For a long time Damon stretched out on his bed, staring at the pattern of swirling craters of texture on the ceiling. Then he got his baseball glove from where it hung from a hook on the wall and lay back down. He put the glove over his face, breathing through the webbing, taking in the sweet smell of saddle-soaped leather. This was his Enos Slaughter glove, now dark-worn and supple. He pulled the glove down from his face and pounded his fist into its deep pocket. Then he held his fist there, his fingernails cutting into his palms, his fist clenched and white and hidden while he waited for what might happen next.

Chapter 6

BACK IN HALEY, Wallace stopped at home only long enough to drop Boyd off for his car. Wallace wasn't ready to face Iris. He eased back into town and stopped by the church. From the car Wallace watched the construction crew begin to frame one wall of the addition.

Progress at the church was slow—the educational wing, just a slab, was out to one side with a few spindly ends of re-bar sticking out. The church building proper had been built in the 1920s when Haley blossomed from a quick burst of cotton money before the relentless wilting began. Somewhere they had found brick of deep, mottled purple, wanting the church to be different, perhaps, from all of the red brick buildings in town.

The color wasn't bad, as it turned out, but the church itself had been designed with all the flair of a squat county courthouse annex—an afterthought of a building. The builder would have fit in well if he had made it to the 1950s, right at home erecting flat-roofed commercial buildings on the fringes of Dallas.

Churches should reach towards the heavens, Wallace believed. They needed more than a simple wooden cross and frosted windows. But the building was not really important, not its looks, anyway. He was only transferring his general grumpiness and dissatisfaction to something inert. The weather's fault, maybe, all of this drizzle, these low clouds.

He waited in his Dodge and watched for a few minutes more, every once in a while catching himself drumming the top of the steering wheel with his fingers. The three-man crew struggled to raise the frame of a side wall into place—the nailed-together two-by-fours wobbling this way and that as they tilted it up. Wallace expected the whole thing to come apart and crash.

When they had it secured, Wallace stepped out and picked his way across the ground, moving from gravel spills to dry concrete patties that had dripped from the cement truck last week.

What a relief to have dropped Boyd off at his car, a double relief for Wallace not to have stopped and encountered Iris once again in the kitchen.

What had gotten into Damon, anyway? Just when things had half a chance to settle down, he starts bouncing here and there, totally unpredictable. Hormones churning up, Wallace guessed. Absolutely natural. But he resented the disruption, resented the likelihood that Iris would push him into one of those out-behind-the-barn, man-to-man situations with his son. The facts of life, and all that. Lord Almighty, give me strength, he thought. How can I explain what I don't yet understand?

This was hopeless, Wallace thought. He glanced over the work site, taking in the gray, puddled slab, and the odds and ends of knotty, warped boards, and the torn-edged rolls of felt paper. Off to one side were two huge stacks of not-quite-matching purplish brick. This will never get done, Wallace thought.

Eddie Bledsoe, the one-eyed lead carpenter, eased down the

last rung of a stepladder and slid his hammer into a loop in his nail apron. He stiffly limped toward Wallace who stopped and waited, trying to gather up what little inner strength he had. "I guess we'll have rain all winter," Wallace said, somewhat too cheerily.

His comment drew a pessimistic shake of the head from Eddie, but he rolled and licked—then crimped and lit—a cigarette before he said anything. He wore striped overalls and steel-toed boots. His hard-hat was creased across the top, a souvenir from his roughneck days.

"Slow going," Eddie said. "No sir, the rain don't help, neither. We're gonna knock it off in a bit. Christmas Eve, you know. And this weather."

Wallace nodded. He had resigned himself to the local pace of work. Almost. But a few more points on the IQ scale—and a little less cigarette rolling and studying of the plans—would help. He wondered why they didn't just put their minds and bodies to the task and work while they were here. But he kept quiet.

"Had us some vandals last night," Eddie said. He turned back towards the slab, pointed his smoke at a pile of boards laying every which way across the ground. "We're missing a few two-by-fours, I figure. Junior says he can tell. Not many. A few."

"You mean someone stole some boards from us?" Wallace felt resentment rising and his spirits simultaneously falling. "You mean they stole from the church?"

Eddie shrugged. He held the cigarette in his lips, let it dangle down, oblivious to its drooping ash. He pulled a bandana from his pocket and with a fluid movement—a magician's sleight of hand—he had his glass eye in his palm, polishing it with his bandana. "Probably kids," he said. "You might mention it to Buddy Bounds. Those two-by-fours might end up in a vacant lot, or down the hole in somebody's outhouse. You can't tell about kids these days."

Then it struck Wallace—the two-by-four that Sheriff Carter

mentioned this morning, the charred two-by-four at the county dump. He nodded to Eddie who had got his eye almost back in place, a little out of line so that it stared blankly over Wallace's shoulder. "Okay, I'll make sure that Buddy hears about this," Wallace assured him, and moved to the church.

Wallace didn't waste a phone call on Buddy Bounds. This was important—and sure enough, not twenty minutes later Sheriff Carter and a big-chested deputy drove up. Before long they had isolated some shoe prints that led from the street to the lumber pile and back to the street.

"Two or three of these prints will do," the Sheriff said. "We'll send them off to Dallas to the lab." He and Wallace watched while the deputy photographed the prints, the carpenters intently watching the flash, watching the big deputy strain to get as close as he could to the wet ground without kneeling. "But I can tell you right now they'll match. Prints here and out on the highway and at the dump. A one-eyed man could see they're all the same."

Both men glanced over at Eddie, who leaned against the framed-up piece of a wall, his one good eye cocked towards the deputy, a cup of coffee in his hand. "Sorry about that," Sheriff Carter said.

"What now?" Wallace asked, smothering a smile.

"Right now, like I said before, keep your nose to the ground. Let me know what you hear." He leaned close to Wallace. "This has been a big help."

He stopped for a minute. "If you're comfortable enough, you might sit in at the funeral. I'd like to know what that colored preacher has in mind. We don't want trouble around here, folks gettin' out of line, you know. I hear that the Dallas coloreds got their dander up, some already showed up. Probably a bunch more Wednesday, for the funeral."

Wallace shook his head. "That sounds like trouble. Is there something I can do?"

Sheriff Carter shrugged. "The funeral's at two. You'll be done here at church the day after Christmas. Like I say, maybe you could go, but only if you're able. It would be a nice gesture, something that I would appreciate." He waited a moment. "A gesture that would not go unnoticed, I bet."

The sheriff's last words took Wallace by surprise, as if this plain-talking country sheriff had a straight line of sight into Wallace's soul, as if he had taken aim and pulled the trigger that would motivate Wallace to act. Well, Wallace would fool him. Press and publicity aside, he simply would not go. He figured Boyd would go. He would let Boyd make a fool of himself in Southtown—all by himself.

"Well, Christmas is my busiest time of the year," Wallace said. "I have an obligation to my congregation. And to my family, you know."

"Just give it some thought," Sheriff Carter said. He moved towards his car where the deputy waited. He stopped and scraped the mud from his boots on the car's bumper.

Sheriff Carter started the car. He sat for a minute with the door open. Then he got out again, moved back towards Wallace, who met him halfway. "Make me a list sometime, Reverend. The half-dozen most likely candidates for trouble in Haley. Older boys, young men. Misfits, bullies, whatever. I'm not asking you to tell me stories out of school, you understand. But I figure you know the troublemakers."

"Still eyeing the locals?" Wallace asked.

"This was an ad hoc deal. The Klan drives into town and finds a two-by-four and knocks off a colored man—a cripple and a drunk at that? No way. And that was no cross-burning at the dump. The Klan would have left a sign. The board would have been a cross, for sure, and been left out front of the Southtown church, or upright at the side of the road. It was locals, amateurs, I bet. A list from you might help."

"Sure," Wallace shrugged. "Whatever I can do."

"Hope you can be there Wednesday," Sheriff Carter said. "Could make things a whole lot easier. On all of us."

But by now Wallace was hardly listening. His mind had drifted to the list of young men who were troublemakers, likely candidates for mischief. Iris's words ran through his mind. "That Davis boy is a bully, and the Babcocks are trash."

Billy Ray Davis and Royce Babcock. They would be right up there at the top of the list. But they couldn't have been involved. They were with Farris last night, over in Corsicana. With Farris and Damon. Damon had told him that.

"What time did this happen?" Wallace asked. "When was that poor man struck down and killed?"

"Can't tell for sure. It had to be after dark. My guess is probably before Tyner's Store closed at nine. Between seven and nine is my best guess. Coroner may have his own idea, though." He looked at Wallace, his head cocked in a questioning angle, and waited. But Wallace had no more to say, no more questions to ask. Not for Sheriff Carter. Not right now.

After the sheriff and his deputy pulled away, Wallace stood there for a few minutes. A puzzle kept running through his head. There was a pattern to the puzzle, he knew, and not many pieces to work with. There were the boys—his nephew Farris, and Billy Ray, and Royce. And Damon, of course. There was the time, last night from seven or so until nine, and there was Damon, acting strange, not being himself at all.

And however Wallace configured the puzzle, the pieces seemed to fit only one way. The picture emerged clear. Frantically, he went back over the details—the four boys, a long evening out, the time not accounted for, and Damon, afterwards, not being Damon at all. He kept moving the pieces around, but always the pieces fit only that one way.

"Oh, no," he said, shaking his head. He stood there a minute, letting his thoughts run to Billy Ray Davis and Royce Babcock. And then, quick-fire, on to his nephew Farris, and on to that place where everything inevitably led.

"Lord help me," Wallace whispered. He sank to one knee on the soggy ground, not to pray, but drawn down by the weight that now hung in his heart.

"Kin I help you, Reverend?" Eddie hollered from across the way. "You all right?"

Wallace pushed to his feet. He half-turned and nodded. Then he shook his head, jammed his hands deep in his pockets and moved away.

Chapter 7

WALLACE HURRIED IN from the carport and right into the kitchen. He stopped. Iris was chopping onions and celery for tomorrow's cornbread dressing. "You missed lunch," she said, not looking up. The chopping stayed steady, deliberate. "Nell and I are going over to Corsicana for a while. One of us has to finish up the Christmas shopping, you know. And Boyd Douglas called. He wants to set up a time for you two to go to Southtown tomorrow. I reminded him that tomorrow was Christmas Day, that the Methodists celebrate Christmas with a church service, and that you hadn't said a word to me about going down there. He'll call later, but we need to talk about that. We have our own family, you know. And you've got to talk to Damon about his attitude, and now his mouth. I can't believe what he said, right in front of me. I think it's from hanging around with Farris. You know..."

But Wallace was past her and down the hall. He stopped at Damon's closed bedroom door, his hand on the door knob for a moment before he pushed it open.

Damon, prompted by his daddy's questions, told the truth without hesitation, without elaboration. For Damon the world by now had moved off some distance, to a place where he could see what he had done quite clearly, and soon the story flowed steadily from him.

Wallace sat on the edge of Damon's bed and listened, his shoulders slumped forward. His arms rested on his thighs, his hands worked slowly, bringing his fingertips together and then apart and then together again—each time Wallace lined his fingers up perfectly so that the tips lightly touched. He stared at the shelf of books on the wall while he listened to his son struggle to tell him. Wallace shook his head from side to side as he listened. Over and over again he shook his head.

Damon told the story. For a few minutes he stayed true to his vow not to lie, but not to answer more than he was asked. But the words gathered their own weight. Despite his clearheaded vow of the night before, they seemed to roll from him on their own and he was unable to stop them, and unable to stop the tears that followed, great spasms that jerked and tore at his gut, and finally gave him some relief.

Still Wallace sat there, too numb to look at Damon, powerless to reach out and hold him or strike him or raise his voice or comfort him. He could only ask the questions he knew he must ask and hear the answers. He fixed his eyes on the book shelf before him, locked onto one book—*The Mystery of the Lost Lagoon*. A silly title, he thought. But he was unable to take his eyes from it. Wallace repeated the title of the book over and over again, thinking it might somehow hold an answer. But it didn't. Finally he asked, "Does anyone else know this?"

Damon shrugged, then shook his head. "Uh-uh," he said, "I don't guess so. Only Farris and Billy Ray and Royce."

"Okay. You have told me," Wallace finally said. "And that's

enough. At least for now. Don't tell anyone else. Not even your mother."

"What are you going to do?" Damon asked. He pulled his T-shirt up, wiped at his eyes, then his nose. "What will happen? Will I go to jail?"

"Well, I will have to tell the truth. You know that, son. What you boys did—and I know it wasn't you, not your idea—was terribly wrong. Terribly, terribly wrong. And I don't know what will happen," Wallace said. "But jail? No, I don't think so." But Wallace wasn't sure of that.

"It's hard," Damon finally said. Now that his sobbing was over, he wanted to explain himself if he could. "You know, being the preacher's son. I mean you're not bad, not a bad father or anything, but the boys tease me. They think I'm a sissy or a chicken. Or that maybe I'll be a snitch, or something. And I guess I am."

Wallace felt himself sink. "I hate that, son," he said. He wanted to strike back, ask Damon, "Should I be blamed for choosing to be a preacher?" But he knew that wasn't for his son to answer.

So Wallace left, slipping through the living room and out the front door, avoiding the kitchen with its Christmas dinner smells, avoiding Iris and her questions. He drove into town and slowed at the bank, which had closed at noon. A lawyer of sorts officed next door, but he was a pedestrian sort of lawyer, one who made out land deeds and wills and collected hot checks for the bank. He would be no help.

Down the street Wallace drove past the giant Santa Claus, pulling around the cars that crept along underneath. A few words to Sheriff Carter seemed to be the logical next step. So Wallace drove to the church and slowed his car. The carpenters were gone. Wallace could use the phone in his tiny office. It sounded simple, one quick call and Sheriff Carter would be there within a few minutes. It would be over. Or not quite over.

He tried to think out the consequences: The three older boys might stand trial, he guessed, fifteen or sixteen the legal cutoff age for juveniles. Floyd and Nell would never forgive Damon for telling on Farris. He could hear Floyd now, dismissing the whole thing. "The damned nigger...he had no business...drinking whiskey...should have stayed in his place."

Damon, at twelve, might get off with some kind of probation, or end up in a state home for delinquents. He shook his head. That wouldn't be right. Damon was a good boy. It wasn't his fault.

And there would be other ramifications. Wallace couldn't see staying here in Haley, holding forth from the pulpit. That would be laughable in this small town. But where would he go? His bishop had wearied of Wallace's failures and would probably leave him in limbo, hoping that Wallace would gracefully resign and fade out of the church.

Iris would be shattered. They couldn't stay here. Not with Damon implicating Farris, his own cousin, and those other boys. And simply going to school would be impossible for Damon.

Wallace tried to imagine them packing up, moving on. He thought of Uganda. He knew an ex-seminarian who had gone to Uganda. That would be far enough away. But Iris in Uganda? He couldn't see that. No way. And what did Wallace know, what possible good could he provide for people in Uganda, anyway?

He drove south, past Tyner's store. A padlock secured the front door. Farther along, where the boys struck Willie Lee Brown down, was marked by a faint scar at the side of the road. Only a few tire ruts, some raw-skinned earth, marked the spot. By spring all evidence would have disappeared.

Wallace glanced at the sky. The clouds were breaking up. Christmas Day would be cold and clear. In the morning the church would be filled with Haley's few faithful Methodists bolstered by a flock of Christmas-only Christians. For a moment Wallace panicked. He needed to work on his Christmas sermon. Then he gave a soft laugh and shook his head. Tomorrow's sermon would take care of itself.

He could stop by the Baptist Church and visit with Boyd Douglas. But that would lead to some vague platitudes, and Boyd urging him to pray for guidance. Wallace still spoke silent prayers, but no longer really prayed. Prayer had diminished in importance over the years, just slowly seeped away and out of his soul.

And Boyd might simply turn away. Wallace remembered the look Boyd had given him out on the road south, the way he seemed ready to disclaim Wallace when the highway patrolman had questioned him. Boyd would be no help at all.

As it now stood he and Boyd would drive out to the Southtown church Wednesday afternoon and suffer quietly while their dark-skinned brothers and sisters in the Lord wailed and wept and sang and prayed and laid Willie Lee Brown to rest. Wallace and Boyd would be expected to speak up, to lay their holy words on those poor folks, urging the Reverend James Henry Brown to forget his anger and put his trust in the Lord. "Vengeance is mine, sayeth the Lord." The words came easily to Wallace, slid effortlessly off his tongue. But those words offered not one scrap of comfort. Nor conveyed the truth.

The truth. That was the problem. To tell the truth would destroy everything—his career in the church, his relationship with the town and with most of Iris's kin. His marriage might find this strain too much to sustain it further. Already his toying with the truth had led them here, even though the small lies that he told about that woman in Fort Worth had been lies meant not to betray, but to protect.

And the cost to Damon would be immeasurable, possibly ruin what hopes he had for a productive, useful life.

What would happen if Wallace lied? Or if he simply failed to disclose the truth that he now knew? As a pastor he would be secure, and the bishop might take notice of his peacekeeping efforts in Southtown. That might lead to opportunities elsewhere. Iris would tire of Haley after a while, after Wallace proved himself to her once more. And Damon would survive, learn to live with his dark secret. Wallace could help him with that. Time heals.

Yes, Damon could live with the secret. But could Wallace? Could he face his congregation each week from the pulpit and preach the value of a life lived with honesty and integrity? Preach the value of trusting in the Lord?

And what about justice? Right and wrong? Appropriate punishment for the crime committed? What about the Reverend James Henry Brown and his justifiable anger? What about racism and cruelty? Large questions that Wallace weighed against the love he felt for Damon, his only son. Questions that loomed too large for Wallace to answer.

On the way back to his house Wallace spotted Damon down the side street, in front of the Shaver's house. Damon straddled his bike, watching Jimmy Shaver pump up a low tire. Wallace pulled in near the boys and rolled down his window. Jimmy nodded. Damon walked his bike over to the car.

"How's it going?" Wallace asked—a stupid question, he knew.

Damon shrugged. "Okay, I guess."

"You feel better?"

"I guess so," Damon shrugged again. He did feel lighter, the weight he carried in his gut had lessened, but everything still felt unreal, as if he were trapped inside a discombobulated dream.

"Let's take a ride," Wallace said. Damon nodded and leaned his bike against a light pole.

The two of them rode in silence for a few minutes, Wallace trying to gather his thoughts. "You're not taking me to the jail, are you?" Damon asked, his voice a little shaky.

"Of course not," Wallace said. Oh, my God, no, he thought.

At the high school football field, Wallace found a place in the parking lot where the gravel hadn't worn thin. He stopped the car. For a few minutes the two of them stared straight ahead in silence. Everything was gray—the sparse grass of the football field and the damp dirt that showed through the worn spots. The wide-plank bleachers were two tones of gray, dark where the mist had soaked them and lighter underneath, where they stayed dry. Creosote poles curved skyward, black against the somber sky.

Finally Wallace spoke. "If you will do exactly as I say, then things will get better. They may not get better right away, but before too long they will. Do you understand?" he asked. Wallace's voice was full and strong and gentle all at once, and Damon nodded, then said, "Yeah, I guess so."

"Okay." Wallace took a deep breath. "This has to—absolutely must—remain a secret between us." He waited to go on until Damon nodded once again. "When you shared that story with me today, you in essence gave it away. You gave it to me and I accepted it, and now it is mine, no longer yours. Do you understand that?"

Damon nodded.

"Well," Wallace said, "you did give me that secret. Didn't you?"

"Yessir. I guess I did."

"So you no longer own that secret. Now it's mine." Wallace shifted in his seat, worked at getting the words that he spoke to his son just right. "For a time I will be gone. I am taking our secret—now *my* secret—with me. I am taking it from you, because you gave it to me this morning—you already know that—and it is no longer yours.

"When I get to my destination, and I'm not absolutely sure where that will be, no one else can ever have that secret. It is mine to control, to use or to hide or to ignore. It's not the sort of thing that a twelve-year-old boy should have to handle. Do you understand?"

Damon nodded and said yessir again. He felt the weight of that secret, that burden pass out of him and to his daddy. He told Wallace that he thought he understood. "But I don't want you to go away," he said.

"I will be back, or you can come to where I am, but only after I have hidden the secret, my secret, where no one else can find it, and where it will never cause harm." Wallace wanted to say, "I promise," but he knew by now that not everything could be promised.

Then Wallace told his son that this agreement was between the two of them only, and that Damon had to give his word that he would tell no one, not his mother or Jimmy. Not anyone. This was terribly important. He must never, ever, tell anyone else what had happened that Sunday night on the road to Southtown.

Damon gave his word. He looked his daddy in the eye and gave his word, for that seemed to be the right thing to do. His daddy never would have asked it otherwise.

The two of them shook hands, as if now they had become equals—two men who had entered into a binding legal agreement.

∴

IT WAS LATE AFTERNOON when Wallace drove away from the house. He had packed light, not feeling a need to carry many things, mostly a box of books and what clothes he owned. He wrote a long letter and left it on the kitchen table where Iris would find it when she got back from shopping. It started out with, "I know you won't understand this..." and it ended with "Love always." He included reasons enough for leaving. Iris didn't have to know them all.

Wallace drove south, stopping at Fairfield for gas and a bag of chips and a coke before turning onto the new highway to Houston. A logical choice, he thought. Where his life had begun. Maybe back in the city he could get a fresh perspective, make a new start.

The drizzle had started once again, now coating the highway with a slick sheen. Up ahead the clouds from the stalled cold front hung low and heavy. Wallace finished the salty chips and the watery coke. He pulled the headlights on, hoping to lighten the gloom. Every few miles the highway crossed under an overpass supported by round, concrete pillars. Sometimes a pickup truck would be pulled over, stopped under the protection of the overpass, a traveler out in the mist re-tying a tarp that had flapped loose. Cars passed him, hurrying towards the city, with bright Christmas packages crammed behind their back seats.

Those pillars, round and smooth and solid, caught the beam of the car lights now, and Wallace let his mind drift back to the story Damon had told him. He tried to imagine how Damon had felt, riding in the front seat of that Chevrolet, spotting Willie Lee Brown as he trudged down the side of the road. Damon would have swayed a little, then braced himself as Farris swerved to the right, the tires grabbing the gravel, kicking up the dirt at the edge of the road. Wallace, without really thinking, began to edge onto the broad shoulder of the highway, his own tires whining on the rough texture as he eased close to the pillars he passed, as if he were Farris and the pillars were Willie Lee Brown. It evolved into a game of sorts for Wallace, seeing how close he could come to the pillars without hitting one.

He thought about smacking a pillar head-on. He wondered if he would feel the impact. The blow that killed Willie Lee Brown caught that poor man suddenly, by surprise, and he was sedated somewhat by the pint of whiskey—a decided advantage.

Ramming a pillar would take care of the ragged edges of

Wallace's life. He gave an uneasy laugh. Damon's secret would die with him, the puny life insurance policy he had paid on every month for years would provide Iris a decent start on a new life.

He was outside of Houston maybe forty miles now and the overpasses and their concrete pillars became more frequent. Ten or fifteen more ahead of him before he made it to the edge of the city, where he would...what? He hadn't thought that far into the future. Where would he spend the night? What would he do tomorrow? Christmas Day, alone in some cheap motel, he guessed.

The next overpass loomed ahead on his right and he turned the wheel, floorboarded the accelerator and headed straight towards it. His tires whined as they moved across the rough shoulder of the road. Wallace had never felt so calm, so alive. He lined the hood ornament up with the center of the pillar. At the last possible second, with one-handed flair, he jerked the car back to the left and onto the smooth surface of the highway again. But he had felt the tick of metal bumper as it grazed the concrete.

For a moment he was jubilant. Not with the fact that he had touched the pillar with his car, or that he had touched the pillar with his car and survived. No, his jubilation came from somewhere deeper, and a feeling of grace swept through him.

This was his gift. His Christmas gift. There were a dozen pillars still to go. A dozen pillars to aim for between here and Houston, and the choice he made as he approached each one was his gift. A gift that was his alone.

And Wallace drove on, speeding into that dark night.

DONLEY WATT—a native of East Texas—has lived in the Lone Star State most all of his life. A man who understands and appreciates the value of work, he has made a living in a number of different ways—a landman in the oil business, the owner of an herb farm, a dean of a community college.

In 1987, at the age of 47, he decided to follow a childhood dream to become a writer. His collection of short stories, *Can You Get There from Here?* won the Texas Institute of Letters' Stephen F. Turner Award for the best first work of fiction in 1994. His novel, *The Journey of Hector Rabinal*, was a finalist for a Western Writers of America Spur Award.

Donley Watt lives in San Antonio with his wife Lynn, and teaches writing at Trinity University.

Date Due

MAY 27 2008			